'Twas the Mystery Before Christmas

AN ADDIE FOSTER MYSTERY BOOK 6

KIMBERLEY O'MALLEY

This is a work of fiction. All names, characters, places, and events are a product of the author's very vivid imagination. Any resemblance to actual persons, events, or places is purely coincidental.

Published by Carolina Blue Publishing, LLC

Copyright 2020, Carolina Blue Publishing, LLC

ISBN: 978-1-946682-26-0

PRAISE FOR
KIMBERLEY O'MALLEY

Death Comes in Threes – Addie Foster Book 1

"This was my first cozy mystery and I have to say I absolutely loved it. Kimberley did an amazing job at keeping me guessing what was coming next. I can't wait to see what happens between Addy and Detective Wolfe cause something has to happen between them!

I also want to know who the man in Addy's dream is. And why those men were after her.

Can't wait for the next book!"

–Under the Cover Book Blog

"This was the first Cozy Mystery and Kimberley knocked it out of the park. I loved Addie and Grey and the two aunties. The detective puts out the vibe he is serious and hard core. But I am sure he has a soft spot for Addie. Hopefully in the next book we will see where the sparks fly for Addy and why these guys were after her. KUDOS to Kimberley for such a great read."

—Wanda Bridget Hickey, Verified Kindle customer

"This was my first Cozy Mystery and I loved it. I was drawn in by Addie and adored Grey. He was such a charming, funny and protective character. I can't wait to find out more in book two. This book is great for rainy days or a light read while you're on holiday."

— Author T. S. Petersen

Dyeing for Change – Addie Foster Book 2

"Love Addie mysteries, but hate that they are such a quick read. And that I have to wait for the next one!"

— Amazon certified customer.

"Another action-packed book. Don't let it being short stop you from reading. You will absolutely love Addie and her BFF, Grey. They're hilarious. Can't forgot our hottie detective, Jonah. Meow! Trouble is always finding our Addie. She doesn't listen, at all, even if it's for her own good. She loves her dogs, and this book made me shed some tears because of one of her dogs. You can't go wrong with this awesome book. Read the first and then come devour the second."

— Sara, Amazon Kindle customer

"I am really liking this series! A nice, easy and quick read - just enough to take a break from real life and spend a lazy hour or so with a good read. Likeable characters and a continuing mysterious thread involving the main character throughout the two books so far - looking forward to seeing what happens in Book #3!"

— Vivian F. Shane, Amazon Kindle customer

Murder by Numbers – Addie Foster Book 3

"Murder by Numbers by Kimberley O'Malley is the third book in the author's Addie Foster Mystery series. This installment finds our beloved Addie still dealing with her bad dreams, and finding it difficult to avoid trouble. When her estate sale book purchase turns out to be more than she bargained for, she has to solve the mystery before she winds up toes up. This series is full of quirky characters, mystery, and plenty of fun reading."

— Dee, Words That Sparkle

"Wow if mystery is what you're looking for this book has it. This is the third book and Addie seems to find things that get her into trouble. She love estate sales and she found a book that she thought was very different. After purchasing this book she starts to get followed by this creepy English guy who turns out to want that book and is threatening all her family if he doesn't get it. The Author keep you looking for clues and wanting to know how this is going to end. It was an easy fun read."

— TX Shadow

Angel of Death - Addie Foster Book 4

"I think this is my favorite Addie Foster book! Addie and Jonah are a cute couple. He's all alpha protective and she is bubbly and I know I shouldn't do this but I'm going to anyway when it comes to mysteries. Everyone needs a gay bff like Grey. He's someone who you can depend on to be there and will always make you laugh. I love the 2 aunts who worry about her aging eggs lol and of course the two smiling dogs. The suspense is great and laughs are plenty in this one."

— Carolyn, Verified Amazon Customer

"Addie, Grey and the aunts are on the road again. A friend of Addie's wants her to help find out what happened to the elderly man. With a stalker, it adds mystery to the story. The story was great with enough suspense to cause you to want to finish the book. Great read."

— R.W. Verified Amazon Customer

"Someone recommended the first book in the series yesterday, so I grabbed that one last night. At 3:30 this morning, I finished book 3! Loving this series, highly recommended!"

— Kindle Customer

Death by Chocolate-Addie Foster Book 5

"I love this quirky series and I would definitely recommend it to everyone!! Addie always seems to find herself in trouble, even when she's being good and not looking for it. Murder, mystery, drama, protective other half, the aunties and her BFF is just some of the goodness you get from this series. I can't wait for the next book in this series!!"

—Devil Dog Mom, verified Amazon customer

"This was a Great Story again. A good 5th book for this series. I really enjoy these Fun Cozy Mysteries starring Addie Foster. I have read the 1st 4 books in this series and will be re-reading them."

—Linda M., verified Amazon customer

What a way to go, right? Death by Chocolate was an interesting read with some twists and turns. Kimberley O'Malley's book was a page turner. Even though I didn't read the others in the series, it was easy to follow and pick up on all the characters. Now I have to read the others to find out about the 'stalker.' I would definitely recommend this book.

—Author Ester Lopez

Happy Holidays to the world. After all we've endured in 2020, we deserve a little joy and peace!

Chapter One

Addie turned her head from side to side, her ebony curls bouncing with the movement. Something flashed at the edge of vision, catching her attention. Through the murky darkness of the room, light from a streetlamp glinted off something in the corner. She edged closer, hugging her arms to herself to ease the chill that enveloped her body. But it wasn't the type of cold rubbing her arms would ease. This chill came from the fear that weaved its way around her heart and through her chest, threatening to steal her last breath. She wasn't alone in the room...

"How nice of you to join me, Miss Foster," came a voice from the shadows. A hideous laugh followed, its hollow ring sending a torrent of fresh chills down her spine. "Not that you had much of a choice."

Addie pressed herself against the wall. She needed to buy a little time for Jonah or any of the

Ocean Grove PD to arrive. Then she'd be all right.

Before she could shrink far enough into the shadows, a hand snaked out, wrapping itself around her wrist like a manacle.

"Where do you think you're going?" Venom dripped from the disembodied voice, all traces of humor gone.

"No!" Addie screamed. She bolted upright in bed. As the terror of the nightmare released its grip on her, she ran a shaky hand through her sweat-soaked curls.

"Jonah, it's started again," she cried.

Only silence met her announcement. Addie turned her head. Instead of his warm, comforting body, her gaze found a note placed on his pillow.

She read the brief missive and laughed out loud. Jonah had joined Grey, her BFF, at an early morning estate sale in South Carolina. Jonah at an estate sale? The thought brought giggles from her. The thought of Grey at one made her laugh harder. No matter how she begged, she had managed to drag him to only one. And that was years ago. Something about the "musty stench of those places" offended him.

And Jonah, her big, bad detective, was at one with him? Hard to believe. She shook her head at such a thought. Leaning over the edge of her bed, Addie grabbed a pen and small notebook from the single drawer in her bedside table. When the frightening dreams/visions had started last year, she'd taken to journaling the details before she even left her bed to capture them all.

When she finished, Addie left her bed, stretching her back as she pulled open her bedroom door.

"Woof!"

"There you are, my lovely girls!" Addie cried before gathering Gracey and Lily, her two Shetland Sheepdogs, close to her. The wriggling, furry bodies never failed to charm her. Two pink tongues swiped across her face and hands, shoving the last dredges of her nightmare into the recesses of her brain.

She straightened and headed for the kitchen while both dogs ran ahead, yipping with excitement. Addie laughed as they "led" her to their empty food bowls. "I'm not falling for that old trick, my girls," she crooned to them.

Their rule was, whoever got up first fed and walked the girls. Obviously, they'd thought they could trick her into a second breakfast. Instead, Addie opened the fridge and thought about her own. She pulled out the makings for an omelet, one of the few things she could cook without the threat of poisoning herself. As she cracked some eggs over a bowl, her mind drifted back to Jonah's note. Even though the weekend before Christmas guaranteed a plethora of such events, she still couldn't picture her guys at one.

Sharp barks and the girls racing to her front door cut short her musing. One sharp knock confirmed a visitor. Addie glanced down at her flannel PJs and decided she was decent enough to answer it. In light of her still unknown stalker, she peeked around the privacy panel first. A smile creased her face at the sight of her until recently unknown father on the porch.

"Robert, please come in," she called to him after opening the door. They had decided she would call him by his given name rather than his title of her father. At least for now.

"Good morning, darling," Robert greeted her as he came inside. He rubbed his bare hands together. "I must say, it's a bit colder out than I imagined when I set off this morning."

His faint British accent always pleased her. Since she learned of him last spring, and after he survived a near fatal gunshot wound trying to protect her from Jonah's former partner—of all people—she and Robert Martin had begun building a relationship. After all, they had her entire life to catch up on.

"Have you eaten yet? I'm just starting an omelet for myself." Two sharp yips from the girls made her laugh. "And by that, I mean of course the girls will each get a sample."

As if they understood her words, Lily and Gracey raced back to the kitchen.

Robert laughed at their antics.

"Thank you, but I've already eaten. However, I wouldn't turn down a cup of tea on such a chilly morning. And since you're kind enough to stock my favorite one, I'll make the tea while you finish making your breakfast." He grabbed a tin of Harney and Sons Royal English Breakfast Tea.

"Sounds like a plan," Addie responded, getting back to her omelet.

She took a moment to watch Robert, *her father,* move around the kitchen, already familiar with its layout. A grin lit her face. She'd never had a father, or at least known of him, and Addie had given up that particular dream years ago. The few times she'd ever asked first her mother and then later her Aunties, she'd been politely but firmly shut down. After a few tries, she'd given up.

Grey had bugged her for years about searching for her father on the Internet. And who knows, her whacky friend may have done so without her. But family had always meant the people you chose, more than the people you were biologically connected to, for Addie. And she had never wished to insult her aunts, who had always been there for her. She loved her little family, recently enlarged with the addition of Jonah. And now her father. Addie sniffed back a tear she couldn't blame on the onions she chopped.

"Everything okay, my dear?" Robert inquired.

"Oh, happy tears. I was musing about all the changes in my life recently." She sent him a slightly watery grin. "Just a bit of woolgathering."

"Ah, Julia, your mum, used to accuse me of that. Seems as though you come by it naturally."

"I'm sorry I never got to see the two of you together, Robert." Addie sighed and returned to chopping onions and peppers for her omelet. She felt rather than saw him cross the kitchen toward her.

"As am I," Robert said in a soft voice, laying one hand on her shoulder.

After a moment, his hand fell away as he returned to his kettle. Addie thought she heard him whisper, "So many regrets," but she didn't push for an explanation.

Addie whisked the ingredients into the bowl with the eggs. "I miss Mom, every day. She would have loved Smiling Dog Books."

"Your mother did love a good bookstore, the smaller and more crowded, the better. We spent hours perusing just such places in D.C."

Addie turned in time to catch a glimpse of a faraway look in his eyes. Since finding out his identity, she and Robert had spoken at length about his life and family. What they never discussed much was the time he spent with her mother. Addie didn't wish to press and believed it would all come out in its own time.

Robert shook his head, as if clearing cobwebs from his brain.

"And your mother would have loved Jonah. Would have thought him a proper match for you, my dear."

Addie sighed.

"I've often thought that as well."

"Speaking of your young man, where is Jonah this morning?"

Addie placed some bread in the toaster before answering. "Well, believe it or not, he and Grey are at an estate sale." Her laughter carried across the small kitchen.

"But I thought they both loathed that sort of thing."

"Exactly!" she crowed. "I awoke to a note propped on his pillow informing me they had driven down to one in South Carolina." She flipped the pan and slid a perfect—for her—omelet onto a plate. "That may be code for 'they went Christmas shopping for me.'"

"But Christmas is in a few days. Surely, Jonah wouldn't have waited until now? Grey, maybe."

"And you'd be wrong! Grey starts his shopping in late winter, sometimes earlier. He likes to say he's keeping his eye out for the 'perfect gift.' It's annoying, really. He's pretty much good at everything. And he does give the best gifts."

A chuckle erupted from Robert. "Really? Are we counting the French cooking class turned misadventure in the 'prefect gift' category?"

Addie winced. "No, we are most certainly not."

Thoughts of the ill-fated class last spring came to mind. The night ended in the poisoning death of the chef and led to Robert's almost dying of a gunshot wound to the belly. The memories of those difficult days brought her earlier nightmare back into focus. She shuddered at the sudden chill in the air.

"Are you quite all right, Addie? Your face seems to have lost a bit of color."

Addie forced a smile she knew didn't reach her eyes. It was the best she could do with the earlier terror seeping back into her bones. She needed to talk to Jonah before she shared any of the details with Robert. It was their thing. Jonah always helped her make sense of the clear-as-mud early nightmares. Half a year had passed without the dreaded nightmares, but now they were back, which meant the next mystery waited right around the corner.

Oh, goodie!

"I'm fine, Robert. Just have a lot on my plate for these last few days before Christmas."

She watched his eyes narrow, aware he probably didn't buy her story. It would have to do for now.

The two resorted to small talk about the upcoming holidays over breakfast. When both had finished and the girls had gotten their fair shares of egg, Robert rose and gathered the few dishes.

"I've got this. Why don't you go get ready for work?"

Addie glanced at the microwave clock, shocked a whole hour had gone by. "I'll take you up on that. Erin will be ready for mutiny if I don't get there soon."

"If *we* don't get there soon," Robert corrected gently.

Although her stalker had once again gone back into hibernation, Addie knew better than to rely on that. Between the three guys in her life, they all managed a fluid schedule of making sure Addie was never alone for long periods of time.

"I'm sure you have better things to do this close to Christmas."

"Spending a few hours with my daughter in her lovely bookstore is not exactly a hardship, Addie." He winked at her. "Now, go get ready."

"On it!" she cried, before dashing down the short hallway to her bedroom.

Turning her shower to just-short-of-boiling, Addie let the water blast away the last scraps of fear from the nightmare. No matter what, this would be an amazing Christmas. They were all together. Her father would be here to celebrate with them. *Her father!* Everyone was happy and healthy. What more could she ask for?

Chapter Two

Addie looked toward the door to her shop as the bells over it jingled while announcing yet another customer. Although she loved the madness of Christmas shopping every year, as her bank account certainly did, she was more than a little ready to be done for the day. Her smile spread at the sight of Jonah and Grey approaching. She rushed to them, throwing her arms around her boyfriend.

"Finally! I was beginning to wonder if you'd been lured away by some other estate sale attendee," she joked before placing a smacking kiss on his lips.

"Oh, I'm fine, thanks," called Grey in his fake aggrieved tone. "And since the average person was more geriatric than siren, your man was safe."

"I didn't forget about you, Grey," Addie

admonished before hugging him and bestowing another kiss, this one on the cheek.

Jonah laughed before holding up a hand. "Two words, Addie. Never. Again." He wiped a hand over his face. "How do you stand that madness so often?"

"I quite enjoy it," announced Robert as he rounded the corner of the local history section. "You boys should have included me."

Addie might have laughed at the unspoken dialogue passing between Grey and Jonah. Or how fast their heads whipped around. And she would have laughed if the reason weren't so serious. She let out a long, shaky breath.

"What they're trying to not say aloud, Robert, is that someone had to stay back to babysit me." She held up a finger as all three men tried to deny it. "It's okay. I understand. I don't like it, but I understand."

Jonah closed the gap between them and drew her against his side. "I know you hate this. We all do. But it's not forever, honey." He drove his point home with a sweet kiss to her temple.

"I know, Jonah, and believe me, I look forward to the day I no longer require a bodyguard." She let out a sigh. "You know how much I love Christmas. It's my absolute favorite time of the year. And we have the added bonus of Robert here to celebrate with us." She smiled at her father, delighted when a slight blush painted his cheeks.

Grey laughed.

"Just like summer is your favorite. Right up until fall and everything pumpkin spiced starts. Face it, Addie, you're fickle."

She shook her head even as a laugh escaped her.

"You're not wrong, Grey. But Christmas is different." She shook one finger at him. "Don't give me your fake Scrooge routine. Christmas is special. People are nicer to each other. They slow down a bit. And the twinkling lights and chill in the air make my heart soar."

"Bah humbug," Grey uttered, the words softened with his grin.

"And last Christmas was so great! Jonah and I celebrated our first together. We all ate our weight in food at the Aunties' on Christmas day." She closed her eyes for a brief second. "And the crazy nightmares were absent."

Addie's eyes flew open, horrified at what she had let slip. Maybe, if she were really lucky, no one picked up on it…

"What aren't you telling us?" came from a disgruntled Grey.

"When did you have another nightmare?" Jonah asked as he stroked one hand up and down her arm.

"What is she talking about?" queried Robert.

Addie held up one hand, buying herself a few moments. She then called to Erin who stood across the store in the children's section.

Her part-time helper and full-time graduate student wandered over. "Hey, the gang's all here," she said by way of greeting.

After a murmured round of greetings, Addie turned to Erin. "Could you be a dear and hold down the fort for a few minutes?"

"Of course," Erin agreed. "I'll just hang out with the girls behind the counter."

When Erin made her way in that direction, Addie turned back to the guys. "This way, please."

Not a word was spoken, not even by Grey, as they followed her into the storeroom. Once inside, Addie closed the door.

"Sorry there's nowhere to sit, but my office is way too small for all of us."

"Stop stalling, and spill it, honey," Grey drawled in his patented lack of tact.

"Someone should really get you a filter for Christmas," Jonah muttered before focusing on Addie.

He took her hands in his, rubbing them. Until that moment, Addie hadn't noticed her hands felt like ice. The tiny gesture melted her heart. She gifted him with a small, shaky smile.

"I'm so sorry I wasn't there for you. Take your time. Tell us everything," Jonah prompted.

Addie closed her eyes and recounted the details of the dream in a flat, soft tone. Even now, surrounded by these men in the safety of her store, an icy chill snaked down her spine. She shuddered against it, reluctant to allow fear to get its claws into her again.

"Well that doesn't tell us anything," Grey drawled.

Jonah's glare did nothing other than make her BFF grin.

"Grey, you know the first dream never reveals much in the way of detail," she admonished him.

In the past, the nightmares always presented in the same fashion. They started out of the blue. Sometimes, like now, months had passed since the last one. The first was always vague; just enough to let her know it was starting again. Each successive one grew more detailed.

"How long has this been happening?" asked Robert.

Since the events last spring, Addie had enjoyed a respite from the terrifying dreams. And Robert had never been involved from the beginning. She needed to catch him up.

"Seems like forever, but it's only been about eighteen months, give or take," Grey answered. "You know, the time some Eastern European thugs tried to murder Addie."

"Grey!" Addie yelled. "That's low, even for you."

Robert's face hardened ever so slightly. If Addie hadn't been standing next to him, she may have missed it.

"While lacking tact, he's not wrong," Robert stated.

The group remained silent for a moment as if all lost in thought back to that time. One thing they'd learned since meeting Robert was, those criminals *were* related to him. While unable to reveal exactly his role in the government, much to Grey's chagrin, Robert had admitted to being the cause of that near-fatal event. The thugs had somehow discovered his link to Addie and hoped to use that to weaken him. They had been wrong. Dead wrong.

"Robert, you are not to blame for the choices those men made," Addie exclaimed.

"You're right, of course, but I am the reason they targeted you. And if anything had happened…" His voice trailed off as his eyes closed.

Addie took a step closer to him, placing her hand over his, which he held clenched in a fist.

"But it didn't. And now they're gone and you're here. And none of that was your fault."

"She's right, you know," Grey joked. "Addie has been known to get herself into a bit of a pickle without your help."

Jonah sighed before facing Robert.

"While Grey lacks a filter, he makes up for this with honesty. There have been several incidents since then that held no ties to you." Jonah held the older man's gaze for a moment. "But then I believe you already know this."

"I do indeed," Robert agreed. "Although I kept my distance to ensure your safety,

Adelaide, I always knew what was happening in your life. And when this all started last year, I did the best I could to keep you safe."

Addie smiled up at him.

"And as thankful as I am for that, I'm so much happier to have you here in Ocean Grove, in my life."

"Okay, now that we've had all the feels of a Hallmark Christmas movie, can we get back to the problem at hand?" begged Grey.

Laughter and a few "Oh, Greys" filled the air.

"He's right, you know," Addie said. "With Christmas only a few days away, I'd like to get this over with so we can all enjoy the holiday."

"Not to mention some of Gertie's famous cranberry-apple pie," Grey mentioned.

Jonah's eyes lit, softening his serious expression.

"Oh, that is a good one. But then there's her chocolate malted fudgy peppermint pie. It's hard to top that."

"Both sound wonderful. And if your friend's Christmas desserts come anywhere close to the ones I've already tasted, this will be a holiday to remember." Robert rubbed his stomach to drive home his point.

"All the more reason to get this, whatever it's about to be, over and done with. So, what do we know?" Grey looked at Addie to start.

"Well, I already described the dream.

And as we know, the first in the series never reveals much." Addie twisted her hands together as she spoke.

Jonah took both of her hands in his. "Did you have any sense of being in the space before, Addie? Was anything at all familiar to you?"

"Was there a big neon sign above the man's head, maybe saying his name?" Grey joked.

Addie stuck out her tongue at Grey.

"They never make it that easy, as you know. And no to Jonah as well. Although I could see very little of my surroundings, nothing struck me as familiar. Sorry."

"No worries, Addie. It'll all reveal itself in time."

"Hopefully in time for us to enjoy Christmas," Addie said on a sigh.

Jonah laid an arm around her shoulder, drawing her to his side. "How about for now, we just enjoy the holidays? I happen to have it on good authority the Aunties would love to make dinner for us all tonight."

Addie laughed, and it felt good bubbling out of her and chasing away the previous dread.

"Oh, you do, do you? And whose authority might that be, Jonah?"

"Why, I got it straight from the horse's mouth, so to speak." He slid his phone from his back pocket and brought up a text for all to see.

Addie giggled again when she read the sender. Her aunts, long known for their frugality, insisted on sharing one cellular phone between them. "After all, if someone wants to get ahold of one of us, we're always together," she'd heard them both say a million times.

She leaned in closer and read the body of the text aloud. *"Dinner tonight at eight. Don't be late."*

Addie laughed aloud this time. "Jonah's right. We've been given a command performance."

Robert, who'd been privy to many such meals since moving to Ocean Grove last summer, smiled. "I know better than to say no to that. A missive from the queen wouldn't carry as much weight."

"I never say no to a meal I don't have to cook," Addie joked.

"And by 'cook', she means nuke in a microwave or order take-out," Grey laughed.

"Hey, my girl's an excellent orderer. And when was the last time you broke a sweat cooking, Grey?" Jonah demanded.

"Enough, boys! Some of us still have work to do before this wonderful meal we're all drooling over. Now fight between you to figure out who gets to be my 'watchdog' until I close the shop later. And the others can go bug Gerti's for something sinful for dessert tonight." She waved her hands at the lot, silently shooing them along.

Jonah placed a smacking kiss on her temple. "I'll be catching up on quality time with

Addie," Jonah announced, thus taking the debate out of it. He pulled Addie by the hand out of the storage room and back toward the front counter. "Why don't we relieve Erin? I'm sure she has things she'd rather be doing tonight."

"Aw, aren't you thoughtful?" Addie stretched up onto her toes to bestow a quick kiss on his lips.

"Well, sure, that, too." He wagged his dark eyebrows at her. "How do you know I wasn't just trying to get you alone?"

Addie's laughter rang throughout the store. "Sure, just you and me and all the last-minute shoppers, bless their hearts."

Chapter Three

A few hours later, Addie leaned back in her chair and only barely managed not to groan aloud at the amount of food she'd consumed. She glanced around her Aunties' antique cherry dining room table and smiled at the faces gathered. Despite whatever uncertainties life held in store for her, in this moment she couldn't be more content.

"So, Jonah, have you managed to knock up my grandniece yet?" cackled Clementine from the head of the table.

Okay, correction. She could be even more content without the mention of her "decaying eggs" or references to Jonah's "capability" as they like to call it.

"Aunt Clementine, please! How about a moratorium on any discussions involving the words pregnancy, sperm count, and eggs until the new year? Please? It could be your gift to me this year."

Grey, leaning forward with a devilish glint in his eyes, shook his head.

"I'm still waiting to hear what Jonah has to say."

For his answer, Grey got Jonah's balled up linen napkin in his face. Everyone laughed.

Addie turned to Robert.

"How have you not run screaming for the hills yet? I can't imagine you've ever endured family gatherings quite like ours."

Robert wiped the corners of his mouth before replacing his own napkin across his lap.

"And you'd be right, Addie. Growing up the only child of a diplomat and his wife didn't offer such rousing dinners as I have had the pleasure to experience here. I'm only thankful you've opened up your homes to me after a lifetime of absence."

Addie wrapped one of her hands around his.

"It never occurred to me not to do so."

She sniffed back unshed tears. She spoke the truth. Before he'd ever had a chance to explain, Robert had willingly stepped in front of a bullet to protect her. How could she say no? Much later, when his life was no longer in danger and Robert was well on the road to recovery, they had their heart-to-heart. At least the first of many.

Jonah's hand squeezed her thigh under

the table. Addie sent him a damp smile.

"Julia, your mother, was right to keep your existence from me. My, uh, career made having a normal, family life impossible. She knew that about me from the moment we met. Well, she knew enough to rule out any kind of long-term relationship. And she didn't seem to care. And neither did I." He rubbed a hand over his face. "I knew better than to get involved with her. But the heart wants what it wants, or so they say. From the moment I laid eyes on her, your mother was the only woman for me."

"I know a little something about that," Jonah murmured.

The tears flowed unchecked down Addie's face.

"Oh, Robert, I wish you two could have had your happily ever after."

He shook his head.

"It wasn't meant to be, Adelaide. But this chance I've been given to get to know my beautiful daughter is all I need."

"Just think what a grandchild or two would do for you, Robert," Beatrice shrilled across the table.

Addie merely rolled her eyes, while everyone laughed. Before she could say anything, Grey stood.

"Although goodness knows there's nothing I like better than a good Addie roast, those pies aren't going to devour themselves. Who wants dessert?"

*****

"I got off easily tonight," Jonah drawled as he climbed into bed later that night. "Not even one comment about my underwear preferences."

Addie looked up from the Kindle app on her phone. "You almost sound disappointed."

"Not at all. Just relieved." He turned off the light and slid into his side of the bed. "Besides, there's still Christmas. Want to wager on whether or not I get more boxers?"

Addie laughed as she closed her app and plugged in her phone on the bedside table. "I still wonder how they knew the right size last year."

Jonah shuddered. "Some things don't bear thinking about."

Addie clicked off her light and snuggled up against him, placing her head on his chest.

"You know, instead of making up a story about an estate sale, you could have just told me you were going Christmas shopping."

Her head bobbed against the rumble of laughter in his chest.

"Oh, believe me, Grey and I did indeed go estate sale shopping. I can pull up my maps app to show you if you don't believe me. I'm not sure he'll ever forgive me."

"Sorry for doubting you, but I cannot imagine either of my guys at one, let alone both of you. What could you possibly have said to Grey to get him to agree to go?"

"Uh uh," Jonah admonished. "Didn't your mother ever tell you, no questions at Christmas?"

Addie chuckled. "Uh, no, not really. What does that mean?"

Jonah answered with a laugh of his own. "When we were all young, our mother used to say, 'No questions at Christmas.' We weren't allowed to ask her where she went or what Santa might be bringing. She wanted it all to be a surprise, I guess."

"Should have thought of that for Grey. He's impossible to buy for and always begs for hints right up until Christmas morning."

"I can see where he would be that way. Grey is, uh, different."

Addie smothered a laugh. "That might be the nicest way I've ever heard it put." This time, she smothered a yawn. "Sorry, it's been a long day, and tomorrow will be another one."

Addie's eyes drifted closed as she felt Jonah gather her in his arms. A smile creased her face as he whispered goodnight against her temple.

*****

"Do you know how long I've searched for this? Do you?" The man's voice screeched at an almost ear-splitting decibel. "Only to find out

someone beat me to it! Well, I won't stand for it." He shoved a long, bony hand into Addie's face. *"Give it to me now."*

The gnarled hand, with its twisted and deformed knuckles, made her jump back from him. *"If I had any idea what you were talking about, I'd be happy to return it."*

"Well, if you don't have it, who does?"

In the dim light, Addie could see the man's skin flush.

"I don't have all day, young lady. And I am losing my patience. I NEED it now."

The man banged the floor beneath their feet with his cane. Although he appeared and sounded elderly, the force of the cane banging belied a much younger man. Addie did her best to shrink back away from him before he decided to use the cane on her.

Almost as though he'd read her mind, the man raised it again. This time, the handle appeared in the single source of weak light. The head of a dragon with glowing green eyes appeared in front of Addie's face. For a moment, she couldn't draw her eyes from it.

"Enough!" the man cried as he whipped the cane through the air next to her, smashing glass into smithereens on the floor. *"You will do as I say."*

"No," Addie cried, arms flung out in front to protect herself from the flying glass.

She struggled against a pair of strong hands on her upper arms.

"Let me go. I don't know what you want!" she cried.

"Sweetheart, you had another nightmare.

33

You're okay, Addie," Jonah crooned to her as he gathered her struggling body into his.

Addie's eyes popped open and she stared into his dark brown eyes. Relief flowed through her like a cool stream on a hot summer's day. She collapsed against him, whimpering from the memory of the nightmare.

"Hush now, Addie, I have you. You're safe here." Jonah stroked one hand up and down her back as he continued to whisper to her.

Soft whining coming from the floor drew her attention. Lily and Gracey both crowded the bed, one paw each up on the comforter.

"Good girls," Addie crooned to them as she pet each silky head. "Everything is all right now. Mommy just had a silly dream."

"Maybe 'nightmare' is a better term," Jonah suggested.

He reached around her to pull out the small notebook from the bedside drawer. "You speak, I'll write."

Her heart made a funny little flop in her chest at his kindness. Jonah never complained. He took on the strange specter of her prophetic dreams without even the blink of an eye. How had she gotten so lucky?

Addie closed her eyes and recited everything she could remember. She told him all the details of the cane's handle. For some reason, it seemed important. When she finished, she glanced at her phone for the time and groaned.

"Ugh, I have to get to the shop."

"How about you get ready, and I'll have your coffee ready to go when you leave?"

Addie leaned over and kissed Jonah. "Sounds like a plan. Today is going to be terribly busy if past years are any indication."

Once in the bathroom, Addie twisted the shower control to as hot as she could handle. The nightmares always left her with a chill down to her bones. And while the hot water couldn't completely remove that, it helped. She stepped in, singing a favorite Christmas song at the top of her lungs and way off-key, not that she cared. She'd never quit her day job, but everything about Christmas brought joy to her heart. She wouldn't let the newest series of bad dreams taint it.

Too many minutes later, she cursed under her breath seeing the time on her phone. Even though Grey and Erin had already opened Smiling Dog Books for the day, Addie needed to be there as well. With just a few shopping days left, it was all hands on deck.

The scent of peppermint drew her to the kitchen. Grey might harass her for being predictable, but December, specifically Christmas time, meant peppermint-flavored coffee. Jonah got it, why couldn't Grey?

"I like the fact that you accept my seasonal coffee penchants," she joked with Jonah as she entered the kitchen.

His back was turned to her, and she craned her neck to see what he had hurriedly put in the pocket of his sweats. Jonah turned, with a grin on his face.

"What else would you drink days before Christmas?"

Addie leaned down to sniff the fragrant steam wafting from her travel mug. "Ah! Not sure why Grey always has to bust me about this."

"Maybe because he's Grey?" Jonah suggested.

"True," Addie agreed, taking the smallest sip of her brew.

"And you wouldn't have it any other way," Jonah commented with a laugh.

"Also true. You know me well." She leaned up and kissed his cheek. "As much as I'd love to stay here with you and the girls, it's off to work I go."

"That's right, honey, go make the big bucks, while I stay home and play with the girls."

At his words, Gracey and Lily woofed softly and crowded around their humans.

"I'm okay with that, knowing you couldn't sit home idly for more than a few minutes before you thought of something that needed doing."

Was it her imagination, or did Jonah shift his body so his pocket was out of her view? What was he doing?

The man in question raised a dark brow. "See something you like?" he joked.

Heat filled her face. "You caught me. I, uh, really need to get going."

"Yes, you do. And Grey is meeting you there, right?" Jonah closed the distance between them and kissed her. He then rested his forehead against hers. "Be careful. I'll see you later."

"Yes, and you, too," she answered. Even though he wasn't going to work today, Addie knew just how crazy the world was.

"Always."

Jonah retreated to their bedroom. Addie watched him walk away before screwing on the lid of her travel mug. Between the two of them, they had quite the collection. This one sported a picture of Will Farrell from the movie Elf shouting, "Christmas is my favorite!" It had been a gag gift from Grey a few years back. As much as she loved Christmas, she wasn't a huge fan of the film. Much to her friend's shock and dismay.

She pet both dogs, wishing them a good day. As she left the house, she saw them run down the short hallway to the master bedroom. Funny how easily Jonah had slipped into their routines. The girls always went to work with her. But now, on his days off, Jonah generally kept them with him, sometimes bringing them on errands or dropping them off later with Addie.

Addie left the house, singing a Christmas carol and inhaling the lovely aroma of peppermint coffee. Despite the terrifying specter

of her nightmares, she grinned to herself.
What could possibly go wrong today?

Chapter Four

By mid-afternoon, Addie wished, for maybe a second, she'd chosen a nine-to-five desk job. One that required far less time on her feet and far less patience. A career where no one would ever give her the stink-eye when she couldn't guarantee a rare first-edition book on time for Christmas, five days away.

But then she glanced around her store and saw a young couple with an infant picking out a copy of *Twas the Night Before Christmas.* The mother gushed about continuing the tradition of reading it on Christmas Eve, as her parents had done with her. The husband smiled as he stroked the downy hair of their daughter, who slept in an infant sling on his chest. Addie swallowed a lump in her throat, grateful to be such a small part of their lives.

After ringing up their purchase, she

turned to watch them leave, shaking her head at ever thinking there was a better job for her than this.

"Bet you a dollar the kid throws up all over that book," Grey joked from behind her.

"That's terrible, even for you," Addie accused him with a grin to soften her words. "You're just jealous."

A hearty laugh erupted from him. "Of J-Lo's killer body at fifty, yes I am. Not to mention the fact that she shares a bed with A-Rod. But of having a crying tiny human with sticky fingers and an endless number of dirty diapers? No, ma'am, I am not." He leaned across the counter and pointed in her face. "But you, my dear, have 'baby fever' written all over your adorable face."

Addie allowed herself to dream for a moment about having a baby with Jonah. Would he or she have her curly hair, or his thick, straight locks? Dark chocolate eyes like Jonah or her blue ones? She could so easily picture a miniature version of Jonah running around with the girls.

A hand waved in front of her eyes.

"Earth to Addie. Come in, Addie!" Grey shouted.

She snapped back to the present. A small line had formed at the register, so she got busy checking out customers and chatting with them about the upcoming holidays as she did. Grey's occasional raised brow and frustrated look caused her to giggle several times, knowing he didn't like to wait to finish their conversation.

When the line finally died out, he raced behind the counter.

"Tell me, did I win the pot?"

She blinked at him, having no idea what he meant. "Huh? What pot?"

Grey suddenly developed an intense interest in his buffed nails. "Oh, nothing."

She tapped one booted foot, sighing at her inability to wear flip flops in December. "I've got all day. Tell me now and get it over with."

And then the weirdest thing happened. A dull red crept across Grey's high cheekbones. She gaped. "Are you blushing?"

He cleared his throat. Loudly. "Of course not. What could possibly make me do that?"

"Oh, I don't know. Maybe the thing you still haven't explained to me. The 'pot' you want to win."

He dropped his gaze to the floor exactly as a ghastly thought overcame her. "Did you by any chance bet someone about whether or not I'm pregnant?" Her voice shrilled at the end, causing a number of heads to turn.

Too late, she remembered the store full of customers. And then she thought back to the last time they'd had a similar conversation in this very spot, with a local minister within earshot.

Addie held up her head, refusing to skulk.

"Grey, please answer me."

His head swung up with a stubborn set of

his chin. "It's not like I started it. I, uh, merely joined in."

"Joined in what, exactly?" she asked, toe still tapping.

Grey released a huffy breath. "Well, if you must know, it started down at the Cut 'N Curl. Seems there's a small wager going as to when you might be, uh, in the family way, so to speak." He grinned at her; all traces of embarrassment gone. "I took December, so if you are prego, I win!"

"Are you kidding me?" Back came the shrill sound dogs could probably hear for miles. Addie drew in a breath, closed her eyes, and counted to ten as she prayed for strength. And the wisdom not to kill him.

"Beatrice and Clementine started it," Grey whined.

She opened her eyes. "Of course they did. After all, they aren't 'getting any younger,' as they like to remind me on a daily basis."

"So? Are you?" Grey glanced at her belly.

The hope in his voice made her laugh. The man who had more money than God cared about winning a small pool. Knowing him the way she did, Addie also knew he wanted to win more than he wanted the money. Grey was competitive if nothing else.

"No, Grey, I am not. But thanks for asking."

His lips formed a pout. "Really? Then what's going on there?" He waved a hand around her hips. "Maybe too much seasonal indulgence? I keep telling you to join my gym."

Addie's mouth gaped open. She could feel it. And she was fairly sure she resembled a trout. But she couldn't help it. What had he just said to her?

"Ooh, you're so in the dog-house for that one, Grey," came Jonah's rather amused voice.

Addie turned as Jonah walked behind the desk, led by two prancing Shelties, complete with bells on their collars. She dropped to her knees oohing and aahing over both girls.

"Someone's been to the doggy boutique," she gushed before looking up at Jonah. She ran her fingers over Lily's green collar with bells and Gracey's red one. "To what do we owe this unexpected shopping trip?"

Jonah handed her the leashes and pulled something from his pocket. He handed her a picture of the girls with Santa. "Today's the last day for photos, and all the money goes to the local shelter. How could I say no?"

Addie stood and hugged him. "You're a very sweet man, Jonah Wolfe."

Grey shook his head in mock disgust. "You are whipped is what you are, Detective Wolfe."

Jonah shrugged his large shoulders. "I can live with that."

Addie grinned at Grey's slumped shoulders. "Hey, I know. Why don't you tell him what we were just talking about, Grey?"

His blond brows met his hairline. "No, I don't think that's necessary. And I think someone's calling my name." He held a hand to his ear. "Yep, definitely heard it again."

Addie laughed as he took off into one of the aisles. She then turned back to Jonah.

"You're not going to believe what he's done this time." She shook her head and laughed at the shock she'd be seeing soon on Jonah's face. "Not in a million years."

Jonah cocked his head, as if thinking about the answer. "Is it worse than betting on what month I'd impregnate you?"

And for the second time in less than an hour, Addie's mouth dropped open.

"You knew?" she shrieked. So much for remembering where she was.

"The Aunties tried to get the 'inside scoop,' as Clementine put it."

"Are you kidding me?" But then she shook her head. "Of course they'd do that. Those two are obsessed. And a menace."

"What month does Grey have?" Jonah asked.

"December, as in right now, if you can believe it."

She stifled a laugh as Jonah glanced at her stomach.

"No, Jonah, he didn't win," she said.

"Just kidding. We live together, Addie. It's not like I don't know when you have your period. There's always a run on chocolate," he

44

joked.

"You're not wrong," she answered.

"Have you given any more thought to what the man in your nightmare is seeking?"

"Not too much." She waved an arm toward the crowded space around her. "We've been, thankfully, swamped since I got here. Still, I can't imagine. What could I possibly have worth threatening me over?"

An older woman with a death grip on a little boy's hand approached the counter. "Excuse me. Can you help me find something for Ethan?" She pointed at the little dark-haired boy. "He wants to buy his kindergarten teacher a book for Christmas. Maybe you'd have some ideas."

Addie smothered a laugh at the expression on the woman's face. She came around the counter and squatted down in front of him. "Tell me, Ethan, about your teacher. What does she like?"

His dark eyes shone. "Miss Gilbert loves to read! She reads to us every day. I told Granny I want to buy her a book."

Grandma frowned. "Which is a lovely idea, except how do we know *what* she likes to read?"

"Your grandmother has a point. Tell me how Miss Gilbert decorated her classroom. Does she have posters or pictures on the walls?"

Ethan closed his eyes, as if trying to picture the classroom.

"Animals!" he yelled after a moment. "She has all kinds of animals on the walls. Big ones. Little ones." He burst into giggles. "She even has one of a giraffe. It's so funny looking." He stood on his toes and stretched his arm up as far as he could. "The neck is, like, this tall."

Addie got an idea. "Wait right here. I have just the book."

She strode to the section on animals and ran her finger along the spines, searching for just the right one. Finding it, she plucked it from the shelf and turned back toward the counter. A tall, older man came around the corner and bumped right into Addie.

"Oh, I'm so sorry," she said. "I really have to be more careful."

"No problem, young lady," he demurred.

Something in his tone sent a chill sliding down Addie's spine.

"Did you find a book for Miss Gilbert?" Ethan yelled from the front of the store.

Addie held the book aloft. "I did," she answered.

She turned to get a better look at the old man, but he no longer stood there. Addie heard the jingle of bells over her front door. But when she looked, a number of people entered and exited at the same time. She couldn't tell if he numbered amongst them.

"Which book did you get?" Ethan asked.

Addie shrugged off the bad feeling and rejoined the young boy and his grandmother.

"Well, since your teacher loves animals, I thought of this book."

She held aloft a coffee table style book about zoos across the world. Opening it, she flipped through the pages, showing them the large, glossy photos of animals.

"Do you think Miss Gilbert would like this?" she asked Ethan.

The little boy jumped up and down. "Ooh, she's gonna love this!" He turned to his grandmother. "Can we buy this for her? Pwease?"

"Of course we can, Ethan." She grinned at Addie. "You're a lifesaver. How did you know how to do that? I would have never thought to ask."

Addie laughed and walked around the counter to ring up their purchase. "It comes with the territory. I have a lot of young kids in here for story times. We have some rather interesting conversations."

"Story time? What's that?" asked Ethan, his hazel eyes rounded in his face.

"Story time is when I read a book for kids, Ethan. Different ages come at different times to hear a story." Addie plucked a schedule of events for January, handing it to his grandmother. "This will tell you all the different ones we have each month."

She finished the transaction, handing back her credit card and purchase.

"Here you go, Ethan. It was so nice to

meet you. And Merry Christmas to you both!"

"What do you say, Ethan?" his grandmother prompted the young boy.

"Thank you, ma'am. Happy Christmas to you too. I hope Santa brings you lots of presents!"

Addie laughed along with his grandmother and waved goodbye as they left the store.

She glanced around, trying to spot the man she'd almost collided with. But she couldn't find him. And yet an odd tingling sensation prickled the back of her neck. Addie wondered if he was somewhere close, watching her. The way he'd said "young lady" brought to mind her latest nightmare.

Addie sighed. Jonah would need to know this for sure.

Chapter Five

Jonah's jaw hardened before Addie's eyes as she told him about the man in the store. And possibly her latest round of nightmares. Jonah in detective mode was a force to be reckoned with. She reached out one trembling hand to smooth his jaw. With only days left before Christmas, their most serious question should be canned cranberries (never) or whole. Instead, she told him, again, about the man in the store.

"And you're sure you've never seen him before?" Jonah questioned for the thirty-seven thousandth time, or so it seemed.

She shook her head before restraining wild curls behind both ears. "I barely saw him this time. It all happened in the blink of an eye. One minute, I rounded the corner, crashing into him. The next, Ethan called to me. When I turned back, he was gone."

Jonah bent his head over a small notebook, taking notes as they talked. "So we have average everything and older than us," he stated, with a twinge of disgust in his voice.

"Pretty much," Addie replied.

"How about the walking stick with the dragon handle? Was he holding anything like that?"

Addie squeezed her eyes shut, more to take a break than remember anything. "No, I don't remember seeing anything in his hands other than gloves."

"Gloves? What gloves? You didn't mention gloves." Grey grilled her from his place behind the counter.

"Really?" Addie muttered.

"Do you mind?" Jonah asked at the same time.

"Yes and not at all. Happy to help." Grey's signature smirk dissolved when neither of them responded to his idea of a joke. "Uh, sorry. Addie, weren't you saying something about gloves?"

Jonah gave him the stink-eye before turning back to Addie. "Can you describe the gloves, Addie?"

"I only saw them for a moment. He had on black leather gloves. I remember thinking it was odd. Most people remove their gloves when inside."

Jonah scribbled something. "So no walking stick, then?"

"No, I only saw the gloves," Addie sighed. "Sorry."

"No worries," Jonah said, sliding the notebook into the back pocket of his jeans.

She glanced around, happy to see the store was still mostly full with shoppers. "Let me get back to it. I'd rather stay busy."

"Of course." Jonah kissed her temple before walking away.

Addie couldn't help noticing him catch Grey's eye and nod his head toward the back of the store. She bit her lip, not wanting to know what the two of them were cooking up. Shaking her head, Addie cruised her store, stopping to chat with customers, old and new, and grabbing out of place books to be reshelved.

By closing time, Addie felt more than ready to go home. She watched Grey follow the last customer to the door, flipping the sign and locking the door behind the gentleman.

Although she wanted only a glass of wine and hot bath, or foot massage, Addie grabbed the vacuum from the storage room and began using it. Better to do it now than try to rush things tomorrow morning. Erin had already left for the day. Grey approached her.

"Do you need me for anything? If not, I have a bit of last-minute Christmas stuff to do."

She waved a hand toward the door. "I'll only be a few moments, and Jonah is here." She leaned in to kiss his cheek. "Thank you, as always."

"Of course. See you tomorrow."

Addie watched him disappear into the storage room. His car was parked out back, next to hers. She went back to vacuuming, humming another oldie but goodie Christmas tune. When she finished, she turned off the machine and wrapped up the cord. She turned to see Jonah and Robert deep in conversation on one of the couches in the reading area.

"Hey, guys, I'm done finally."

She grinned at the way the two sprang apart on hearing her. Almost like they had been discussing something they didn't wish for her to hear. Hmmm, what could that be?

"Oh, hey, Addie. I didn't hear you come up," Jonah said, with a bit too much enthusiasm.

She cocked her head and grinned at him. "Was it something I wasn't meant to hear?"

"What?" asked Robert, eyes all wide and innocent. "Of course not. Jonah and I were discussing the menu for Christmas dinner. I imagine it will be similar to Thanksgiving."

She looked from one man to the other. While she doubted his words, she let it pass. After all, as Jonah had told her, you don't ask questions at Christmas.

"To be honest, you can expect even more food. Consider yourself warned."

Robert looked at Jonah who nodded.

"Last year just about killed me. I had to add quite a few miles to my run," Jonah joked.

"And for those of us who don't

run…well, let's just say I'm screwed." Addie patted her hips which would no doubt widen this week.

Jonah pulled her into his arms. "More of you to love!"

She swatted at him. "Remember that when I look like a Christmas heifer."

"You'll be no such thing," Jonah admonished.

Robert smiled at them both and then covered a yawn. "Well, if you don't need me for anything, I'll be on my way." He turned to Jonah. "Since you're back to work tomorrow, I'll be by to gather Adelaide in the morning."

Addie ground her teeth but held her tongue. Even though her stalker had gone radio silent once again, there was no need to be careless.

"Thank you, Robert. And remember, we have the early shift in the morning." She groaned thinking about it. It would feel as though she'd never gone home. But she wouldn't complain. That meant a healthy bank balance at the end of this month.

"As I'm used to being up before the crack of dawn, no problem, my dear. Shall I stop and pick up breakfast on the way?"

"Oh, you don't have to do that," Addie demurred.

"Which is why I'd love to," Robert countered.

"Well, that would be lovely then," she

agreed. "Surprise me."

Robert leaned in and kissed Addie's cheek. "Until tomorrow morning." With a hand raised to Jonah, he left the store.

Addie smiled at her father's retreating back. *Her father!* That would never get old.

Jonah locked the door after Robert before turning back to Addie. "What else can I help you with before we leave?"

She glanced around, not finding anything amiss. "We should be good. Now all we have to do is take the girls out and decide on dinner." She grinned at him. "Whose turn is it to pick?"

Jonah laughed. "We really do need to learn how to cook someday. Can you imagine doing this with little ones?"

Addie's heart swelled, while her ovaries may have just stood up and cheered. "Little ones, huh?"

"Well, I didn't choose a month in the pool, but yeah, little ones."

Her smile grew as she approached Jonah. "How did I ever get so lucky?"

"Same way I did," Jonah answered before wrapping her in his arms. "We still need to decide on dinner," he whispered against her temple.

"Why don't we order something and just take it home with us? It's so chilly at night now, I'd rather eat in front of the fireplace."

"Sounds like a plan. Chinese? Thai? Mexican? Italian?" he suggested.

"You pick, while I run to the bathroom."

Addie strode to the storage room and entered their small employee bathroom. After she took care of business and washed her hands, she stared at her reflection in the mirror. She couldn't help wondering if Jonah's mention of "little ones" meant he was planning on proposing. Theirs had been a far from normal courtship, what with danger around every corner. But they had discussed children as soon as they started dating. Maybe because neither of them was getting any younger. And though thirty-five was far from ancient, she felt the pressure of time. And of her ticking biological clock.

She wondered if he meant to propose at Christmas. It would be hard to top his gift to her last Christmas, a trip to the Caribbean, but a ring would do it. Addie glanced down at her bare left hand, trying to imagine a ring nestled there. Would he go for the obvious choice of a diamond? Or maybe a different stone, something more personal?

Addie shook her head at such thoughts. Whatever Jonah picked would be great, and she'd love it and wear it with pride. She loved the idea of a wedding. Of them standing up in front of all their friends and family to declare their love and intentions. Although it may be a bit old-fashioned these days, they'd agreed early on they both wanted to be married before they brought a child into this world.

"Addie, you okay in there?" Jonah called from just outside the door. "I have the girls ready to go and have called in a takeout order."

"Coming," she called. Good thing he interrupted. Next, she'd be practicing saying "I do" in the mirror. Addie shook her head and opened the door.

*****

"One day, I'll learn to save half of that for another time," Jonah groused. He leaned back into the sofa and groaned.

Addie laughed before looking down at what little remained of her pasta with vodka sauce. "You're not wrong," she muttered. "I feel a food coma coming on."

At the word "food," Lily opened one eye from her spot in front of the fire. When nothing delicious materialized, she closed it again. Gracey slept on with her back to her sister, sharing the warmth of the flames.

"Considering Christmas is only a few days away, we really should be watching what we eat," Jonah suggested.

She glanced at him, stretched back against the cushions, eyes closed.

"Even if we stopped eating now, we'd still not be ready for the massive meal on Christmas. You've already survived one. You know I'm only half-joking."

Jonah opened his eyes. "Oh, I remember."

He sat up straighter, with a sleepy look to his face. "Going into these events, I always think about limiting what I put on my plate." He shook his head. "But who can do that? Between the honey ham and roasted turkey, corn pudding, candied yams, and not one but two types of dressing, not to mention the salads and rolls. Ugh! How can I choose?"

"You forgot the desserts," Addie accused, with a laugh.

"Oh, I didn't forget them. How could I ever forget dessert? There's always at least three kinds of Gertie's pies, not to mention a few things whipped up by the Aunties. We should have started fasting last week. We're doomed."

"Sure, easy for you to say. All men have to do is add a few miles to their run for a week, and it'll be like Christmas never happened. While I'll have to resort to wearing my fat clothes for a month."

Addie closed her eyes and sighed. She might have said it jokingly, but that's exactly what would happen. *It's not fair.*

"You could always take up running with me," Jonah suggested.

Addie laughed and laughed. She wiped her eyes before noticing he hadn't been laughing with her.

"Oh, you were serious? Me? Running?" Another snort of laughter escaped her.

"Why is that such an odd idea?"

Before she thought better of it, Addie

dashed off a quick text to Grey with Jonah's idea. She only waited a moment before he replied with a GIF of Phoebe from the TV show *Friends*, running in Central Park. It set her off howling again.

Jonah picked up her phone and laughed when he saw it.

"I think you could do better than that. After all, you'd have your own personal trainer with you."

"Stop," she said on a wheeze, holding her arms across her ribs. "Can't. Breathe." Her shoulders continued to shake even as she tried to get herself together.

"I'm serious, Addie. I could make you into a runner."

"Oh, Jonah, you're so sweet. No, but thank you. I have been thinking of joining a water aerobics class at the local Y. Mrs. Henry swears by it. Says it helped to 'get her groove back' after her injury last fall."

Jonah made a face. "Do I want to know what that means?"

"Probably not. But I would be the youngest person there."

"By decades, I imagine," Jonah said.

Addie felt her face flaming at the other reason Mrs. Henry had suggested the class. She turned away from Jonah under the guise of grabbing her glass of Diet Mt. Dew. She stretched and yawned as the long day caught up with her.

"Out with it," suggested Jonah with laughter in his voice.

Addie faced him, eyes widened. "Out with what, honey?"

"Whatever else Mrs. Henry said to you about joining her class. You should never play poker."

"Don't be mad. Promise me you won't be mad."

Jonah made an X over his heart. "Whatever it is can't be that bad, Addie. The longer you take to tell me, the worse it seems."

"You're right." She took a deep breath and blew it out. "So, Mrs. Henry told me, as if it would be enticing, there were plenty of single men in the class. And this is a direct quote. 'If that young man of yours doesn't learn to fish or cut bait, then we'll find you someone who can.'"

Addie didn't say anything else, waiting for his reaction. She didn't have to wait long.

Jonah burst out laughing. The kind of laughter that makes you double over and gasp for breath. A full-on holding your ribs in case they break kind of laughter. A laughter so loud, it brought the girls from their slumber to crowd around Jonah, sniffing and whining.

When he finally gained control, Jonah looked at her. "You tell Mrs. Henry I love to fish."

Chapter Six

"If you don't have it, then that man does. No matter to me. What's mine is mine, and you'll take me to him," the man growled at her.

The dim light shone on the metal of the small gun in his hand. Addie gasped. If only she knew what he was talking about, then maybe she could figure a way out of this mess. Knowing she was on her own at the moment, Addie slowed her breathing. She focused only on the man and small but lethal looking gun in his hand.

"Maybe we could turn on a light? Pull up a chair, and then you could explain to me what it is you're talking about. You keep saying 'it,' but I have no idea what it might be."

But if the hardening of his features meant anything, her attempt had failed.

"Do you think I'm stupid, young lady?" he growled at Addie.

"O-o-of c-c-course n-n-not," she replied, clenching both hands together. She didn't want to show any fear. Or at least any more fear.

"He bought it at an estate sale in South Carolina last weekend." The man stopped, cocked his head, and stared at Addie, as though trying to figure out a riddle. "Humph, maybe you don't know. Neither here nor there. He has what's mine. And I will get it back."

Before Addie could reply, the man closed the space between them until the metal of his gun stabbed into her ribs. Time was running out.

"Ouch!" Addie yelled as she sat straight up in bed. Her wide eyes took in the cheerful décor of her bedroom and early morning sunshine streaming in. Her heart slowed its gallop as reality seeped back into her consciousness.

Lily bounded into the bedroom and leapt on the bed. She pushed her silky muzzle under one of Addie's shaking hands, as if offering doggy support.

"What a good girl," Addie crooned to her sweet dog.

Gracey raced in a second later, with Jonah on her heels. The graceful dog joined her sister on the bed and licked Addie's face.

"Honey, what happened?" asked Jonah.

She noticed he was already dressed for work. Addie reached for her notebook and scribbled as she spoke.

"He's escalated, Jonah. I felt his… I'm not

sure how to describe it. He was losing patience. It's like he had to have it, whatever it is."

"I heard you yell 'ouch' from all the way in the kitchen. Why? Did he hurt you in the dream?"

Addie dragged one shaky hand across her face. "He had a g-g-gun, Jonah, and he shoved it in my ribs. I could *feel* it. How is that possible?"

Jonah's brows met his hairline.

"I don't know, Addie, but these dreams have always been your area, not mine. What else happened?"

Addie bit her lower lip, gnawing at the sensitive skin until she was sure blood would appear. She dropped her gaze from his.

Jonah entered the room fully and sat next to her. He took her hands in his, blowing on her chilly ones.

"Whatever it is, honey, you have to tell me. No secrets, remember?"

Addie counted to ten in her head before meeting his gaze again. In his dark chocolate eyes she saw only love and concern.

"At first, he said if I didn't have it, and I have no idea still what 'it' is, then 'that man does.' I didn't understand. Until…"

Jonah pressed a kiss to her fingertips.

"Until?" he prompted gently.

She blew out a breath.

"Until he said, 'he bought it at an estate sale in South Carolina last weekend,' Jonah. That means either you or Grey."

She watched the color bleed from Jonah's face even as his eyes hardened.

"Did he say anything else? Anything at all?"

She nodded. "The last thing he said was something like, 'He has something of mine. I want it back.' What could that possibly mean? Did either of you buy anything last weekend?"

Addie watched as he dropped his gaze from hers.

"Jonah? What aren't you telling me?" Addie ran a hand along his jaw, the morning stubble tickling her palm. "Tell me, please."

"Grey and I both bought a few things. We were, uh, Christmas shopping. Not sure how to tell which of the items this man refers to."

Addie stared into his eyes, trying to tease out the subtext of his words. Jonah never hesitated or avoided her gaze. *What was he not telling her?*

"Not sure. Maybe if I saw the items, something would come to me?" Addie knew she grasped at straws but didn't know what else to do.

"And the man never said which guy? I mean, it could have been either of us." Jonah pulled his phone from the pocket of his dress pants. "Let me text Grey."

A pit opened in her stomach as she watched Jonah walk across the room, his back to her, as his fingers flew over his phone's keyboard. *What was going on?*

He turned back to her as he slid his phone back into his pocket. "Let's see if Grey has any ideas. Are you going to be okay? I have to get in early. Odd timing, but today is Natalie's first day as a detective."

"Oh, that's right. I'm so excited for her. She deserves it."

And Addie meant it. After talking at length with the younger woman over a pitcher of margaritas last summer, Addie finally put away her insecurity. Especially after Natalie had laughed until tears ran down her face at the idea that she had a thing for Jonah. The officer had assured Addie, repeatedly, she looked up to Jonah on a professional level and hoped make detective one day soon. Flashing a beautiful engagement ring she didn't wear while working helped seal it. Natalie had gotten engaged to Sean, a local firefighter, with whom she'd grown up. They planned a beach wedding for the next summer.

Jonah grinned. "I'm so glad you no longer think there's anything between me and her. It would have made us being partners a bit difficult." He winked at her as he straightened his tie.

Addie felt the heat rise in her cheeks.

"Please don't remind me of my foolishness. But you can see where I would have worried, Jonah. She's beautiful and younger than me."

"I really can't. You're the only one for me,

Addie. Have been pretty much since I first laid eyes on you. That's not going to change."

Addie rolled her eyes. This was an old argument for them.

"Oh, that's right. Seeing me covered in a man's blood turned you on. And was it the passing out or the part where I vomited on you that sealed the deal? Ooh, I know! Maybe the thinking I had murdered someone."

Jonah huffed out a laugh.

"We've been over this. I never believed you murdered that thug. The passing out pretty much took care of that idea. It was your sassiness that caught my eye."

"Well, in my defense, who wants a hot cop calling them 'ma'am?'"

Her words only caused Jonah to grin.

"So you thought I was hot, huh?"

A knock at the front door and the subsequent crazed barking of two overprotective Shelties save her from answering.

"That'll be Robert. Why don't you jump in the shower while I let him in?" Jonah kissed her. "I'll see you later. We'll try to stop by the store. I know Natalie misses you."

"That works for me. Tell Robert I need only twenty minutes."

"I will. I already fed the girls, so he can let them out while he waits. Have a great day, honey."

"You, too," she called to his retreating back.

Glancing at the time, Addie realized Jonah was late leaving. And that meant she would be late if she didn't hurry. She and Robert needed to open the store today. Well, she would open it, and Robert would play guard dog.

She rushed through her shower and dressed, choosing her ugliest of ugly Christmas sweaters. Grey would gag when he saw it and, as usual, chastise her for wearing it in public. Which was half the fun. Each year, she tried to make the week before Christmas as fun as possible, both for her and her customers. She held different events, such as making holiday crafts with the kids who came in and free candy cane day, where customers got one made at the candy shop down the block with each purchase.

Over the past few years, these traditions had grown in popularity with her customers. On the Saturday after Thanksgiving, also known as Small Business Saturday, Addie posted a calendar of that year's Christmas events in the store and sent it out in an email blast. By far, the most fun and well received event was The Day of the Ugly Christmas Sweater, much to Grey's chagrin and horror. He would be scarce today, as he refused to be "seen in such an abomination," as he reminded her every year.

Addie drew the sweater over her head, stopping to glance in the bathroom mirror. She burst out laughing at her reflection. This year's entry might just take the cake. The red was nothing short of garish and sported a wreath with a reindeer head sticking through it on the front. The actual wreath and reindeer stood out from the background. The wreath was constructed of some sort of artificial greenery, while the reindeer was a stuffed animal or at least the head of it. She turned and glanced over her shoulder to see the words "Do You Want to Play Some Reindeer Games" in large green letters on her back.

She slipped festive bell earrings in her ears and left the bedroom. She only made it to the edge of the kitchen before stopping in wonder. There stood Robert, her very proper British father, wearing an equally hideous Christmas sweater. She could only stare as laughter poured from her.

"Will I quite do?" he asked, modeling his sweater for her.

Addie needed several long moments to be able to answer him. His ugly sweater sported the words "The Year Without a Santa Claus" and a Santa mug shot.

"Jonah helped me pick this," Robert added.

"I can see that," she managed before another wave of giggles overtook her.

"I'm rather excited for Grey to see it. He has such good taste in clothing. Such style, that one."

"Please stop. I need to breathe," she implored him.

"I like yours," he added, pointing at

Dancer, or maybe Dasher, seemingly jumping from the front of her sweater.

Addie wiped the tears from her face.

"Grey will never forgive me when he sees you," she told Robert.

Robert looked down at his own sweater, then back up at her, with a shrewd grin on his face.

"He won't be sporting something similar?"

She shook her head as laughter overtook her again.

"If at all possible, Grey will avoid even entering Smiling Dog Books today," she clarified.

A definite gleam entered his eyes.

"We'll see about that, now won't we?" He smiled at Addie before crossing to the slider and letting in the girls. "Are you about ready to go, my dear?"

"I am. Let me just grab my things," she answered.

A few minutes later, they started the brief drive to the store. As Robert drove, Addie shared the details of the latest dream. What she didn't expect was the rather evil chuckle from him. She turned to glance at him.

"What am I missing?"

"It's all about the cat." He laughed at the look on her face.

"What cat?" Addie asked.

"'Curiosity killed the cat, but satisfaction

brought it back.' Your friend Grey will never be able to resist getting involved once he hears about your dream. I predict he will be at Smiling Dog Books today after all."

Chapter Seven

With only three days until Christmas Eve, Smiling Dogs enjoyed a robust sales day. Ugly Christmas Sweater Day didn't hurt. Addie manned her post behind the counter, ringing up sale after sale. People could say all they wanted about e-readers. Today's traffic said otherwise.

She watched Robert chat with an older couple as he showed them to the section containing cookbooks. After his recovery last summer, Robert had started coming to the store. And while at first it was to spend time with her, he came to enjoy it. Addie knew he must be bored after a lifetime of doing, well, whatever he had been doing. The details remained a bit fuzzy. She had the funny feeling they always would.

Robert approached the counter once she finished ringing up the latest round of customers. He grinned and held up his phone.

"I texted Grey, giving him just enough details to reel him in," Robert told her, laughing.

"You're evil, but I love it. I cannot wait to see his face when he sees what you're wearing."

As in previous years, her Day of the Ugly Christmas Sweater was a hit. Anyone spotted wearing one received a ten percent discount on all purchases that day. And while that certainly helped, Addie also knew her customers loved getting into the spirit of it. Both the young and old arrived, sporting all kinds of crazy, ugly sweaters. Addie took pictures of the most outrageous ones to post on the store website.

Another round of customers swarmed the counter, ready to check out. Robert, with a wave of his hand, set off to help others find what they sought. Almost an hour passed before Addie caught a bit of a breather. She heard the bells over the door and looked up in time to catch Grey striding in. She couldn't wait to see his expression when he caught sight of Robert's sweater.

"Addie, really? Again? What will it take to drive some fashion sense into that thick skull of yours?" he lamented.

Addie bit her tongue as Robert came up behind Grey.

"Not sure there's any hope. It may prove genetic."

Grey swung toward Robert. His mouth fell open, and for once he remained silent. All he could do was point at Robert's chest and gasp.

Erin joined them at the counter. She waved at Grey before turning her attention to Robert.

"I didn't get a chance to tell you earlier. Good one, Mr. Martin. I've heard many customers murmuring about your ugly sweater."

"Oh, Addie, what have you done?" Grey cried. "You've taken this dashing Englishman and turned him into, well, I'm not quite sure what. How could you?"

Addie pointed at Grey's pouting face.

"Robert, if you've ever wondered what he looked like as a young boy, here you go."

Her father laughed.

"He does rather resemble a young child who's had his favorite toy taken away from him. Cheer up, Grey, Ugly Sweater Day will be over in a few hours."

"Thank all that is holy," Grey enthused. He then narrowed his eyes. "You lured me here under false pretenses."

"Not at all, my friend. We do need to discuss your shopping trip with Jonah." Robert looked around him before leaning in closer. "Something about that day has caught the attention of this man. In order for Addie to remain safe, we must find out what."

"For whatever reason, Jonah is being secretive about this. He has some crazy notion that I'll find out about something he bought.

Does he really think I don't already know?"

"You do?" squeaked Grey.

"How do you know?" Robert asked at the same time.

Addie glanced from one man to the other. *Why was everyone acting so weird?*

"Of course I know. He knows how much I enjoy estate sales. Obviously, he got me something for Christmas."

She paused when both men shared a look she couldn't decipher.

"Does he really think my finding out about a Christmas gift a few days early will make a huge difference? Can you imagine being upset about that? I mean, really! This is my safety we're talking about!"

"Christmas gift! Of course," Grey said.

"I imagine your young man just wants whatever it is to be a surprise, Adelaide," Robert added.

Addie dragged a hand through her wild curls.

"I get it. I do. But maybe this year he'll have to get over it. Maybe if I can see what y'all bought, I might have some idea of what the man is seeking. How else can we solve this and get on with Christmas?"

Robert and Grey shared another look before turning back to her.

"Well, since Jonah is working today, why don't I run home and fetch the two things I bought?"

Addie opened her mouth to agree when the bell rang over the door.

"Hope you didn't start Ugly Christmas Sweater Day without us," bellowed Aunt Beatrice as she made her way to the counter.

Addie squinted and wished for sunglasses. Her aunt wore a sweater with more flashing lights than some houses had. She thanked her lucky stars she wasn't prone to seizures.

"Hey, Aunt Beatrice. That sure is some sweater you're wearing."

It would have been more accurate to say the sweater wore her, but Addie had been raised better than that. There didn't seem to be any particular design or theme, unless as-bright-as-possible counted.

"Ahem," sounded from behind Beatrice.

Addie laughed as her aunt Clementine strode out from behind her sister.

"Don't forget about me," she cackled. "At least my ugly sweater makes you laugh."

Grey let out a hoot as he eyed her sweater.

"Why, Aunt Clementine, is Santa doing what I think he's doing?" he drawled.

"Everyone poops, young man," she answered, with a cackle of her own.

And sure enough, Santa sat over a chimney, red, furry pants down around his ankles, while he read a newspaper. Nothing much left to the imagination.

"Oh, my," Addie breathed. "That sure is, uh, interesting."

She whipped her head around, hoping there weren't many small kids nearby. She chose her words very carefully.

"Yours might not be the most family friendly, Aunt Clementine," Addie suggested as she crossed her fingers behind her back for good luck. One never knew how either of the Aunties might react in any situation.

Clementine threw back her head and roared, ensuring the attention of everyone within earshot.

"My darling girl, everyone poops! Even Santa."

"Did that lady just say, 'Santa poops?'" a small tow-headed boy asked his parents who were busy steering him away from Aunt Clementine.

"Yes, of course they do, but maybe we don't have to announce it quite so loudly," Addie suggested in a stage whisper.

"Aunt Clementine, if I didn't know better, I'd think your one and only grandniece just shushed you," Grey insinuated.

"Really, Grey? Maybe I should shush you!" Addie countered.

Clementine clapped her hands.

"Children, that is more than enough!" Clementine admonished.

Addie felt the heat spread across her cheeks.

"She knows we're not actually children anymore, right?" Grey asked loudly for all to hear.

Robert chuckled.

Addie tried to make herself as small as possible.

Clementine fixed Grey with a steely gaze.

"Perhaps if you acted your age and not your shoe size, Grey, I wouldn't need to address you in such a manner."

"Sister, they are in their thirties," Beatrice reminded her.

"Yes, I am aware. Then maybe they should act that age."

Feeling a tingle on her neck, Addie looked over her shoulder. A man stood outside, staring at her. She couldn't be sure, but he looked like the man from yesterday, and possibly her dreams.

"Uh, excuse me a moment," she called before dashing around the counter and out the front door.

But by the time she made it outside, the man was nowhere to be seen. *Had it been her imagination?*

"Addie, what happened?"

She turned to see Grey and Robert approaching her. Both wore matching expressions. Brows drawn down and frowns. She glanced back to the sidewalk one final time, but the man was gone.

"It's nothing, really. I thought I saw him

again."

Both frowns deepened.

"Him, as in the man from your nightmare?" Robert asked in a tight voice.

"She's impossible that way. You'll get used to it," advised Grey. "She's forever forgetting about her own safety and dashing off here and there to solve the riddle of her latest nightmares."

"And look how well that ended last time," drawled Robert.

Addie fisted her hands and placed them on her hips.

"I'm right here," she reminded them.

"Yes, dear, we can see you." Robert placed a hand on her shoulder. "Why don't we go back inside and see what Grey brought for us to see?"

Addie released a long breath. *Finally, something constructive to do.*

"What an excellent idea!"

She spun on her heel and marched toward the door, trying to remember these two men loved her. That's why they insisted on treating her as though she might be brain damaged.

After ensuring Erin could handle the counter and escorting the Aunties to their car, the three gathered in her tiny office. Addie cleared some debris from the two visitor chairs before collapsing in her own desk chair.

Grey placed a bag on the floor at his feet

before reaching inside and pulling out something.

"This is for my father." He placed a pocket watch on the desk.

Addie picked it up, turning it over and over in her hands. The piece was gorgeous and obviously antique.

"Your dad will love this, Grey." She handed it to Robert to inspect.

"Without knowing your father, I would have to agree. This is beautiful and so well cared for."

"So, Addie, get any 'feelings' when you held it? Is this what the man seeks?" Grey couldn't finish the question without laughing.

Robert looked back and forth between them.

"Am I missing something?"

Addie shook her head.

"Grey doesn't want to believe my 'psychic powers,' as he puts it, are limited to my weird prophetic dreams."

"Well, wouldn't it be great if she could predict lottery numbers?" Grey asked.

"As if you don't already have more money than God."

Robert burst out laughing, drawing both of their attention.

"What?" he asked, wiping his eyes. "You really do sound like children. Or an old married couple."

"Except she lacks the proper plumbing."

"And we'd kill each other," Addie said. She glanced at Grey. "No, I didn't 'feel' anything."

"Darn!"

"What else do you have?" Robert asked him.

"I only bought one other thing." He reached back in and extracted a fountain pen and inkwell.

"Wow, those are pretty," Addie breathed. She twirled the pen in her hand. "I take it this is for your mother?"

"Good guess." He turned to Robert. "Mom has a thing for antique fountain pens. She has a huge collection. Finding this was a coup."

"Although I have no idea why the man in my nightmare is so intent on getting his hands on whatever he thinks we have, I'm not sure either of these things is it. I mean I guess they could be. Maybe one of these belonged to an ancestor."

"It's possible," Grey agreed.

"Or maybe he's after something Jonah bought," Addie suggested. "So spill it, Grey."

Chapter Eight

Grey's eyes bulged out like that of a cartoon character. After a moment, she watched him school his features. A slight smile and bored look replaced it.

"I can't imagine anything Jonah bought would incur such interest. After all, Jonah isn't exactly known for his taste."

"Grey, play nice. Oh, and nice try, by the way."

"He's lying, you know," Robert observed. "Notice the way he bit his lower lip? That's Grey's tell. He does that when he's lying or nervous."

"Great! Now the former spy is tattling on me."

"You're only annoyed because he's right," Addie said, with a laugh. "Now, what aren't you telling me, Grey?"

But her oldest friend made the motion of locking his lip and tossing away the key.

"It's no use, Robert. Grey is as stubborn as they come."

Her father merely raised one brow.

"I believe I could make him tell us," he said in such a calm tone, the hairs on the back of Addie's neck stood up.

"I don't think that'll be necessary, Robert. I'll speak with Jonah again tonight. Make him see the error of his ways."

Grey hitched a thumb in Robert's direction. "If not, there's always the thumb screws."

"Funny." Addie stood. "I think we've left Erin alone for long enough. It was worth a shot looking at what you'd bought. I just wish I knew what he meant. How else can we figure out this problem?"

*****

Hours later, Robert pulled into her driveway. He parked next to Jonah's truck. "I see your young man is home. I'll watch until you get inside."

"Are you sure you don't want to come in for dinner? I mean, it won't be a feast like the Aunties serve up, but the company is always good."

"Thank you, but no. I'm looking forward to some downtime after today. While I love that you enjoy such success, the last-minute Christmas rush proved a bit exhausting."

"That I can understand. I can't wait to take off my shoes." She leaned across the front seat and kissed his cheek. "Thank you so much for today."

"Of course, my darling. And I'll see you tomorrow."

"You will. And sleep in, since Grey will be picking me up."

"Maybe I'll do just that. Not getting any younger."

Addie laugh at his self-deprecation. Robert was in better shape than any of them, except maybe Jonah.

"Goodnight, then," she called, getting out to open the back door for the girls.

Addie grabbed their leashes and her stuff and walked to the front porch. She wasn't even halfway there when the front door opened. Jonah smiled and greeted her at the edge of the porch.

"Let me help you," he offered.

They both waved to Robert before going inside.

"I've only been home a few minutes. How does a hot bath sound before dinner? I'll feed the girls and order a pizza."

Addie stretched up on her toes to kiss him.

"That sounds amazing!"

At the word "dinner," the girls raced into

the kitchen dragging their leashes behind them.

"Guess they liked my plan also," Jonah joked. "So, pineapple for you?"

"As if you have to ask."

Addie headed into their bedroom, stopping only to drop her clothing into the hamper. On days like today, she loved a hot bath to give her aching muscles a break. She poured some salts into the steaming water and removed the little makeup she'd worn before slipping into the water.

"Ahhhhh," she moaned aloud to the empty room.

Laying her head against the back of the tub, Addie wondered for God only knew how many times how she'd gotten so lucky in Jonah. He was a good man who treated her well and respected her dreams. What more could she ask for?

Maybe what he'd bought at the estate sale?

She chuckled to herself at the thought. While it might not prove helpful, she couldn't help thinking she really needed to know. The question remained why he hadn't told her. Almost like he was hiding something. But that wasn't his style. Jonah was as straightforward as they came. They shared that quality.

Speak of the devil...

"I brought you a glass of red," Jonah murmured before setting it on the floor next to the tub. "Need me to wash your back?"

Addie laughed as she took a sip of wine.

"Not unless you want to eat cold pizza."

Jonah tilted his head and smiled at her. The smile that always set free a thousand butterflies in her belly.

"If I remember correctly, we have a history with cold pizza."

She smiled at the memory.

"Grey was so pissed that you like pineapple on your pizza, too," she reminisced.

"I can tolerate pineapple on my pizza. It was you I liked," he corrected in a husky tone. "I'm going to change before the delivery guy gets here."

Addie's toes curled under the bubbles. She wondered if there would ever come a day when he didn't affect her like that. She hoped not. She sank back into the mountain of bubbles and thought again about the man from her nightmare. He sought a specific item, which could easily be the pocket watch or fountain pen Grey showed them earlier. And just as likely, it may not be either of them. What if it was something Jonah had purchased?

She mulled this over, while the water grew chilly. By the time she heard the doorbell, her stomach rumbled in anticipation of her favorite pizza. Addie quickly finished her bath, dried off and threw on some old, comfy sweats. By the time she reached the kitchen, Jonah had the table set and pizza box open. And even though she knew he'd fed them, Gracey and Lily sat at his feet, eyes round and tongues lolling out of their mouths.

"Don't let them fool you," Jonah joked. "I've already fed them. Not a single nugget of kibble left." He took her plate and placed a slice on it.

Addie laughed before taking a bite and moaning with pleasure.

"Not my first time at the rodeo. They'd love for me to believe you'd forgotten them." She glanced down at both dogs. "Wouldn't you, girls?"

Both dogs looked up at Addie, their innocent expressions making her laugh.

"Nice try," she told them.

"So, how was your day?" Jonah asked her in between huge bites of his pizza. "I meant to bring Natalie by, but the day got away from us."

"Very busy, but also interesting."

"Oh? How so?"

"Robert got Grey to come in on Ugly Sweater Day. And then there were the ones my Aunties wore." Addie shook her head. "Probably better you missed that part."

"I can only imagine. But Grey? Really? Even I know he hates Ugly Sweater Day and refuses to partake. How'd Robert manage that feat?"

"I'm glad you asked," Addie said with a smirk. "He mentioned to Grey if I were to see the items he'd bought at the estate sale, I might be able to 'read' something from them. You know, see if he had the item the man in my nightmare seeks." She took a drink of her wine to let that information sit for a moment. "And you know how much he wants to believe I have other psychic abilities. He fell for it."

But instead of sharing the joke, Jonah broke off little pieces of his crust and tossed them to the two happy Shelties sitting at his feet.

"Jonah, did you hear me?"

"What? Oh, yes, of course. I take it you didn't get any 'vibes,' so to speak."

"Not a one. And even though it's a long shot, I suggested doing the same with whatever you bought last weekend."

Jonah, who had his glass of water raised to his mouth, made a choking noise.

"I don't think there's any point to that. Do you? After all, you didn't pick up anything from Grey's purchases. And mine are much less interesting."

"Grey felt the same. Said you 'weren't known for your taste.' I told him to play nice."

Jonah laughed, but it sounded forced, not his usual deep chuckle. He shifted in his seat, turning away from her ever so slightly. At first, Addie had found this all funny, what with Jonah and his 'no asking questions at Christmas' rule. But now his body language made her nervous. What could he possibly be hiding? This didn't make any sense.

"Jonah, is there a reason you don't want to tell me?"

Chapter Nine

"No," Jonah muttered before taking his plate to the sink.

"No? That's it? End of discussion? Since when do we do that?"

Addie winced at her tone, but his refusal hurt her.

"I told you no asking questions at Christmas, honey," Jonah said in a lighter tone. "Don't you want to be surprised on Christmas morning?"

Addie flew out of her chair and followed him to the sink. She knew what he was doing; trying to charm her with his good looks and adorable dimples. Well, she wasn't having it. So, she stomped her foot. Of course, wearing shoes might have made more of an impact.

"Don't you try to blind me with your dimples, Jonah Wolfe. I won't have it! What I want is to celebrate Christmas with you and my family without the specter of this strange man hanging over my head."

Jonah turned to face her before drawing her into his arms.

"I know, Addie. And you're right. I was trying not to show you what I got for you, and I lost sight of the bigger picture. I'll be right back."

Addie watched him walk toward their bedroom. Before he'd made it twenty feet, she changed her mind.

"No, Jonah, don't."

He stilled and then turned to face her. "But I thought you wanted to know."

"I did. Well, actually, I didn't. This is ridiculous. I don't want to know what you got me. I love being surprised on Christmas morning. I do want to know what the man in my nightmares is seeking. But looking at whatever you bought won't bring that to fruition. Despite what Grey would have you think, I'm not The Amazing Kreskin. I can't *feel something* from these objects. I certainly can't predict lottery numbers." She shook her head. "One day, I'll learn not to let Grey in my head."

Jonah smiled, a real one that reached his eyes.

"Grey will always get in your head, Addie. That's just the nature of the beast," he added on a laugh.

"You're so right. But it's okay. I know how to mess with him as well." She smothered a yawn. "I know it's early, but I'm exhausted. Tomorrow will be another busy day for sure. I need sleep."

Jonah kissed the top of her head.

"Go get ready for bed. I'll clean up out here and take care of the girls."

Addie wrapped her arms around Jonah. She pressed her cheek against the warm cotton of the T-shirt covering his chest. She inhaled deeply, the crisp scent of him comforting her.

"You really are the best."

Addie headed through their bedroom and into the attached bathroom to get ready for bed. She looked at herself in the mirror, frowning at the shadows under her eyes. She needed sleep. She needed one night without the intrusion of a nightmare. But that was unlikely until they solved this episode.

"I'll ask you one more time, young lady. Where is it?"

The man punctuated his words by banging his heavy walking stick on the floor. Addie tried not to cower, but the dragon's eyes seemed to glow with the man's anger.

"Don't you think I'd tell you if I knew?" she cried out in the murky darkness.

"I don't know why you're lying to me," he bellowed. "It won't save you."

The pressure of the gun in her ribs increased, driving home his point. Addie bit back a sob. Tomorrow was Christmas Eve. She wanted to be with

Jonah and Grey and her family celebrating. Hot tears burned her eyes, but she refused to let them fall. She wouldn't give him the satisfaction. Her mind whirled, seeking an escape from this situation.

A siren then pierced the quiet of the room. Hope stirred within her as it grew closer. Someone was coming. Jonah was coming. He would save her from this man. Icy tendrils of fear gripped at the sound of the man's maniacal laughter.

"You really think he's going to save you? Not without getting what I want. What I need! It's mine, and he doesn't deserve it. Maybe he'll get here in time to watch the life bleed out of you instead."

As the man's laughter filled the room, Addie knew he was losing his grip on reality. She might not have until Jonah got here. Think!

"Think, Addie. Find a way out of here!" Addie yelled.

She felt Jonah's arms around her. He stroked her perspiration-soaked curls.

"I've got you, honey. You're okay," he murmured to her in the darkened bedroom.

With a sob, she turned her face to his chest.

"He h-h-had a g-g-gun, Jonah. I could feel it pressed against my ribs. And his laugh..." A shudder tore through her. "He said he was going to kill me in front of you. He isn't right in the head, Jonah. He sounded so crazy. His laugh sent chills down my spine."

Jonah turned her face until he could look in her eyes. "Tell me what you can remember,

Addie," he implored.

She sat a little straighter and brushed a hand through her damp hair.

"With each dream, he's unravelling. His voice grows shriller. He's edgy, erratic. This time, I could hear a siren growing closer, and all I felt was relief. But then he assured me help would never reach me in time. And if I didn't 'give him what was rightfully his,' he'd kill me in front of you. How does he know about us? I know I've never seen him before. At least not before this week."

"I don't know, Addie. I take it he still hasn't mentioned what it is."

She shook her head and sighed.

"How can we figure this out if we don't know what it is? He keeps acting like I know and won't admit it." She let out a shaky breath. "Whatever it is, he's desperate to have it back. If only we knew."

Addie reached into the nightstand drawer and pulled out her notebook. She took a moment to scribble down everything she could remember. The simple act exhausted her.

"I need more sleep," she moaned.

"It's not even three, honey, go back to sleep." Jonah turned off the light and lay back down, pulling her into his arms. When her head came to a rest on his chest, he kissed her temple. "I'm right here, Addie. No one will hurt you. I've got you."

His deep voice promising her safety was

the last thing Addie heard before sleep claimed her.

*****

The next afternoon, Addie eased her tired bones onto the stool behind the counter. She closed her eyes for a moment, seeking a brief respite. After several nights in a row of disturbed sleep, fatigue ate at her.

"Hey, Addie, what's wrong? You don't look so good," a female voice asked.

She opened her eyes and forced a grin for her friend Gertie.

"Gee, thanks. With friends like you…"

Gertie laughed.

"You know what I mean. You look like you haven't been sleeping well."

"Might be because I haven't been sleeping well," Addie joked in reply. She stretched and groaned at the tension in her back and neck. "You're just as busy as I am and yet you look fabulous. If I didn't love you, I might hate you."

Addie didn't exaggerate. Just shy of thirty, her friend the baker could have been a model. Even with a dusting of flour on her forehead, Gertie made heads turn wherever she went.

Gertie laughed and wiped a hand across her forehead, dislodging the flour.

"Good thing you love me, then."

"True. So how can I help you? Are you

joining the throng of crazed last-minute shoppers?"

"Yes and no. I will be later but not until after the bakery closes. I stopped by to see how you were faring with the crush of last-minute gift seekers."

"Well, aren't you cute? This may be the busiest holiday season yet, so I'll take it. Of course, as you know, my feet and lower back are less pleased."

"Girl! Say no more. These dogs are barking by the time I crawl home. Oh, and speaking of dogs, that's the other reason I'm here." Gertie leaned over the counter to smile at Gracey and Lily. "Hello, girls. Have you been good this year? I might just have a treat for you."

The dogs, already excited to hear their friend's voice, woofed softly in response to the word "treat."

Gertie held up a small bag.

"I experimented with a new recipe last night while making another round of pies." She took two dog treats from the bag, one shaped like a wreath, the other like a Santa. She held up the Santa cookie. "Who wants gingerbread?" When Lily whoofed first, Gertie tossed the cookie to her. "That leaves peanut butter for you, Gracey," she said before tossing the wreath to her.

Both dogs took the cookies to the big bed they shared. The sound of happy crunching brought a smile to Addie's face.

"That was very sweet of you. It's not like you didn't have a million other things to do."

"It was nothing. You know how much I love the girls. Besides, it's nice to have my very own taste testers," Gertie joked. She glanced around the store. "I can see you're swamped. Plus, those pies aren't going to bake themselves."

"True," Addie agreed. "Don't forget about Christmas Eve dinner!"

Every Christmas Eve, the Aunties held a potluck at their home. While they insisted on doing all the cooking for Christmas, everyone brought something for this one to give the elderly sisters a break. The usual people came but the guest list also included any of their friends who could come. This year, Gertie and Erin would be joining them.

"As if I could. I'll be there and not a minute late. I like to have some time to look at the 'options.'" Gertie wagged her eyebrows.

"We all need to arrive before Grey. He likes to think he can choose his gift ahead of time," Addie said. "And with this year's theme being 'DIY,' who knows how it'll end?"

Each year, they played a different gift exchange game. And each year, the gifts had to fit a chosen theme. Last year had been gift cards. The year before that was edible. This year everyone groaned when DIY had been drawn from the hat. Grey, being childlike at best, always maneuvered to get the gift he thought might be best, even though they were all wrapped.

"How funny was it last year when Jonah beat him out for the gift certificate to Udderly Delicious?" Gertie asked while laughter spilled from her. "I love Grey, you know I do, but sometimes he acts like a…"

"I believe 'spoiled child' is the phrase you seek," Addie suggested. "Getting the gift card for dry cleaning sent him over the edge."

Both women dissolved into laughter. After a few moments, Addie regained control. But she'd needed this. With all the discussion swirling around the man from her nightmares, the everyday joy of the season had taken a back seat. That stopped here and now!

"And now, back to the grind," Gertie joked as she left.

"See you later. Thanks for coming by," Addie called to her friend as she left. Gertie might joke about "the grind," but Addie knew her friend loved her life. She'd inherited the family-owned bakery from her grandmother and never looked back. People travelled to Ocean Grove just for Gertie's pies. Then she added her line of gourmet dog cookies to make Any Way You Slice It even more successful.

The next few hours flew by as Addie rang up purchase after purchase. Between that and chatting with the customers, most of whom were repeat business, the day passed in the blink of an eye. Robert had shown up to help out. He liked to wander the store, stopping to chat with people. And the customers loved him. She didn't know if it was his upper-class British accent or open, friendly ways, but many people commented on him as Addie rang up their books.

She took a pile of books to be reshelved once Erin took over the register. Walking toward the parenting section in the back corner, the hairs on her neck stood on edge, as if she'd touched a live wire. She looked around her and over her shoulder, but nothing seemed out of place. And yet she couldn't shake the feeling of being watched. Or maybe stalked. *You're being paranoid. Just enjoy the holiday feeling!*

And then a hand landed heavily on her shoulder!

Chapter Ten

A garbled scream erupted from Addie as she whirled to face her attacker. And came face-to-face with Natalie.

The young detective's face flushed a bright red. She held up both hands toward Addie.

"I am so sorry. I didn't mean to scare you. That was stupid of me to touch you without warning. I really am sorry, Addie."

Once her heartrate dropped back into human range, Addie forced herself to smile. Although Natalie had been privy to a few of the "incidents," she did not know about Addie's somewhat clairvoyant nightmares. She and Jonah preferred to keep that fact in the family, so to speak.

"Oh my goodness, Natalie, you don't have anything to apologize for..."

Jonah screaming her name interrupted whatever else Addie might have said. He rounded the corner of the aisle, sliding to a stop in front of her and Natalie.

"Oh, I thought I heard you scream," he mumbled, eyes darting between the two women.

Natalie barked out a laugh. "I'm to blame, Detective Wolfe. I made the mistake of sneaking up on your girlfriend. I might have taken a few years off her life," she replied, with a sheepish grin.

"Natalie, how many times have I told you it's 'Jonah?' We're partners now. You can't wander around calling me 'Detective Wolfe.'"

"Of course, Detective... I mean, Jonah. Sorry."

"If anyone should apologize, it's me," Addie declared. "I acted like a serial killer had me in their sights."

"Well, I should never have snuck up on you," Natalie offered. "I mentioned to Jonah earlier I wanted to get a book on the history of local firefighting for Sean. He said you could help me."

"Of course I can. Follow me, Natalie."

Addie led the other woman to the appropriate section inviting her to browse and let Addie know if she had any further questions.

"We'll be up front," Addie mentioned as she grabbed Jonah by the sleeve of his jacket.

She took the long way, circling around the back of the store to a relatively deserted corner.

"She's going to think I'm nuts," Addie hissed in a whisper to him.

"Not gonna lie. I thought something happened when I heard you scream. Did she really scare you that badly?"

"Natalie put her hand on my shoulder from behind. And normally, that'd be no big deal."

"But?"

Addie sighed and rubbed her eyes. The lack of sleep wasn't helping.

"But just before she did so, I had the weirdest feeling of being watched. You know where the hair stands up on the back of your neck?"

Jonah nodded. Because of course they both knew she had more than her share of feeling as though someone watched her.

"Did you see the guy again?" Jonah asked.

"No. I looked around sure I would, but nothing. And then Natalie startled me." The corners of her lips drooped. "Gertie came by earlier, and we talked about Christmas Eve and how much fun it is. I don't want this man ruining it for me. For us." Her voice dropped off at the end as she fought the tears burning her lids.

"Hey, look at me," Jonah commanded. He lifted her chin until her gaze met his. "No one is going to ruin Christmas Eve. We are going to eat too much. There will be the inevitable discussion of your ovaries and/or my sperm." Addie giggled at that. "And then, by all that's holy, I will take the prize Grey wants most again this year. I mean, I've been kind of looking forward to that since last Christmas Eve."

Addie's giggle turned into a full-blown belly laugh. Bless this man for not only loving her, but keeping her sane. When the stress of the situation got to her, Addie could always depend on Jonah to have her back and cheer her up.

"I hope you know how much I love you, Jonah Wolfe," she declared.

"I do, Addie Foster, I certainly do."

A few tears slipped down her cheeks. She didn't try to stop them.

"Okay, good." Addie sniffed. "And speaking of Christmas Eve, you and I need to come up with our contribution to the pot-luck. Like, now. We can't wait until the day of, as we did last year."

"There was nothing wrong with the nachos we brought." He couldn't quite say it with a straight face, dissolving into laughter by the end.

"I loved them and thought they added an international flavor to the occasion. But I may have been the only one thinking that. This year — and by this year — I mean two days from now- we should try for something a little more Christmasy."

"We should definitely decide by tonight.

That way we can make sure we buy whatever it is on time." Jonah laughed. "Speaking of Christmas Eve, I may have invited Natalie which means Natalie and Sean. Do you think that'll be okay?"

"What a great idea! You know the Aunties will enjoy a broader audience. And it gives Grey fresh meat to torture in the gift exchange."

Jonah groaned. "Ugh! I didn't think this through. What if they start talking about my sperm count in front of my brand-new partner?"

Addie burst out laughing.

"What do you mean 'if?' You know they will. They really cannot help themselves. But I'm sure you'll be fine. Natalie's not the type to hold that over you. Well, at least not for too long."

"Natalie is exactly that type," Jonah muttered.

"What type am I exactly?" the woman in question asked.

Addie jolted.

"We're going to have to put a bell on you, Natalie. Jonah was telling me you and your fiancé are joining us on Christmas Eve. And I mentioned you better be the crafty type, as the annual gift exchange is meant to be something DIY this year."

"Nice save," Jonah mouthed over his partner's head.

Natalie clapped her hands and jumped up and down.

"I'm exactly that type! I love everything DIY. In fact, Sean and I bought a house a few months ago that requires a lot of work. That's where all our spare time goes. But this is easier. I can whip up something in no time." She clapped her hands again. "Oh, I'm so excited."

"Were you able to find a book for Sean?" Addie asked.

Natalie pulled one from under her arm and held it up to show them.

"This is perfect! It's a history of the fire service here in Ocean Grove. Sean is the third generation in his family to be a firefighter here, so he'll love this!"

"Oh, I'm so glad," Addie enthused. "Come up front with me, and I'll get you on your way."

"Hey, guys!" Grey shouted by way of greeting.

Jonah looked at him and then back at Addie and Natalie.

"Why don't you take care of Natalie? I have something to discuss with Grey for a moment. I'll be right there."

Without waiting for an answer, Jonah nodded to Grey before the two men stepped outside the store. Addie watched them talk as she led Natalie to the counter. While their friendship meant everything to her, Addie couldn't help being intrigued by the sudden need for a conference. Even now, both looked through the window, their eyes quickly darting away when she made eye contact with them.

Odd...

"I just love Grey. He cracks me up," Natalie commented.

"Yes, he sure can be funny when he wants to be."

Addie regaled her with a few anecdotes of their misspent high school days while she rang up the purchase.

Natalie's eyes widened at the last tale.

"How did he ever get the principal's car in the school swimming pool?"

"To this day, I have no idea. He didn't want me to get in trouble with him. Luckily, Grey has as much charm as his family has money. For the cost of a renovated football stadium, he was allowed to graduate with me that spring."

Addie shook her head at the memory of her crazy friend's actions. Never a dull moment.

The bells over the door announced Jonah and Grey returning.

"No worries, man, I got you covered," she overheard her BFF tell her boyfriend. She wondered what that could possibly mean.

"Are you ready?" Jonah asked Natalie.

"I am. Thanks, Addie, for helping me out with this. Sean will love it! See you later."

Jonah stepped around the counter to give Addie a quick kiss then, squatted down to pet the girls.

"I'll see you at home. Don't forget to come

up with a great pot-luck idea."

He waved and was gone before she could answer.

"So no nachos this year?" Grey joked.

"I liked them," Addie protested.

"As did I. However, your Aunties are dyed-in-the-wool Southern ladies. Nachos aren't their idea of a Christmas pot-luck item, my dear."

"I know," she answered on a sigh. "Which is why I am now racking my brain for something to bring this year. You know I'm helpless with anything culinary."

"More like hopeless," Grey joked while dodging the light punch she attempted. "Truth hurts, dear."

"I know," she answered. "What are you bringing this year?"

Like everything else he did, Grey excelled at pot-luck. Not that he cooked any more than she did. But he always managed to show up with something fabulous and never lost a moment's sleep over it. She hated him!

"Well, I'd tell you, but then I'd have to kill you," he smirked and then winced. "Considering how many have tried, that might not have been the best choice of words."

Addie waved a hand, as though joking about her death was nothing. After all, it had become a fairly regular occurrence.

"Since you're no help, again, I'd better start Googling."

"Addie, you haven't even thought about it yet? Christmas Eve is in two days. Two!"

"I am aware, Grey. And since you are no help, you don't get to judge either. And in my defense, I have been a bit busy trying to figure out the latest series of odd and terrifying dreams."

"True. Although the whole someone-is-trying-to-kill-me routine is getting a bit dated," Grey joked.

But Addie had stopped listening. The feeling of eyes burning into her skull had returned. She whirled around, glancing at the people gathered in her bookstore. No one resembled the man she had seen in her dreams. And yet...

"Addie, are you even paying attention?" Grey whined.

She held up a hand and glanced around again. When her back was turned to the front door, she heard the overhead bells jingle. Addie race-walked to the door. She caught a glimpse of a tan overcoat whipping out of sight as she lunged for the handle. She pushed it open, prepared not to let him disappear again, when she ran straight into someone.

Chapter Eleven

Robert caught her, steadying her with his hands on her upper arms.

"Are you okay?" he asked.

"Where is he? Where did he go?" Addie turned this way and that but did not see the man in the overcoat anywhere. "Did you see him?" she asked Robert in a high-pitched, squeaky tone.

Keeping a firm grip on her, Robert led her back into the store before answering.

"Did I seem whom exactly? There wasn't anyone outside when I got here."

Addie ran a hand through her already wild curls, tempted to pull out some.

"How does he keep doing this? One minute he's here. The next he's gone." She rubbed her temples.

"I have no idea, Adelaide. Perhaps we

should call Jonah?"

"No. He and Natalie just left a little bit ago. What would I say? I think the man from my nightmare is back? But he's also invisible? It's not like he's done anything wrong."

"Other than disturb you, of course."

She flashed him a smile.

"Yes, but not exactly punishable by law."

"Guess we'll have to work around that, then," he added without a bit of inflection in his voice.

"A few months ago, Robert, 'working around that' resulted in your trip to the operating room. You almost died. Remember?"

"Yes, of course I remember." He stepped in closer and placed a hand on her shoulder. "And I would do it again without a thought if it meant keeping you safe, Adelaide."

The slight tremble in his voice almost undid her.

"How about this time, no one goes to the operating room? In fact, let's skip the hospital at all costs. What do you say?"

He nodded but didn't respond otherwise, which didn't do much to ease her growing sense of dread. Whatever the dreams meant, she needed to know. And now. No one and nothing would ruin this Christmas for her and her family. She gazed at Robert, and the knowledge that she'd be spending her first ever Christmas with her father flooded her heart with warmth.

"There you are," Grey called on his way

over to them. He nodded at Robert. "Have you given her any good advice? God knows she needs it."

"Advice?" questioned Robert. His eyes cut to Addie. "What advice do you need?"

But before she could answer, Grey laughed aloud.

"Of the culinary kind. As wonderful as our Addie is, cooking is by far not her strong suit. And with Christmas Eve only a few days away, she needs ideas for her contribution to the pot-luck."

"Sadly, she's out of luck if Addie is depending on me for advice in that arena. The only cooking I do is heating things in the microwave, and the best things I make are take-out orders. Sorry."

Grey laughed so hard, he snorted.

"Like father, like daughter, I see."

"Yes, rather," Robert agreed.

And the warmth in her heart spread to the rest of her chest.

*****

By closing time, Addie once again had aching feet but wasn't any closer to figuring out her mystery man. Tomorrow was the day before Christmas Eve, and each heartbeat sounded out more time passing. *Who was the man? What did he want so badly that he plagued her dreams? Had he truly been in her store? Was he watching her?* But all her questions remained unanswered.

She sat in her office, where she'd been banished over an hour ago by Robert and Grey. Apparently, she paced too much and made the customers nervous. She sniffed back tears. While she knew they meant well, it was just another demonstration of how much the mystery man plagued her.

Well, no more!

Addie shut down her laptop and slid it into her carrying case. Gathering her purse, she opened the office door in time to see Robert lock the front door and flip the sign. He turned and smiled when he saw her.

"Feeling any better?"

"Honestly, no. But my 'time out' gave me time to catch up on the dreaded paperwork and time to think." She smiled at his raised brows. "I know I've said it before, but I won't let this man ruin Christmas for me. Having you here to celebrate Christmas with us means everything, Robert. And I won't let him steal the joy from me."

"Good on you. What's the plan?"

"Plan? Now you sound like Grey."

"Hey! I resemble that remark," he joked, joining them.

"I ask because Grey informed me you always have a plan, sometimes even a back-up plan."

Addie laughed, glad for the distraction.

"Well, I try to have a plan. This time, I'm

fresh out. My 'plan' for tonight is to go home, eat Chinese food in front of the television and watch Hallmark Christmas moves. You know, the ones where everything works out in the end."

"And the same handful of actors play the leading roles?" snarked Grey.

Addie rolled her eyes and texted the idea of Chinese for dinner to Jonah. She smiled at his emoji of a thumbs up as his reply.

"Whatever! Who cares? I want to forget for just a little bit if you don't mind. Now, who's taking me home?"

"Should we flip for the pleasure, Robert?" Grey asked, tongue firmly in cheek.

"Not necessary. Adelaide, it would be my pleasure. I'll get the girls organized, while you grab whatever you need."

Addie watched him walk to the counter. She smiled as she overheard him talking with her dogs. While she couldn't make out the words, the crooning quality of his voice made her smile. So much for being a big, bad former whatever he'd been.

"Figure out your pot-luck contribution yet?" Grey asked her, eyes all big and innocent, as if he wasn't actually teasing.

She responded in kind, sticking out her tongue at him.

"I'll get to it," she snarked.

Robert returned holding the leashes of her two prancing Shelties.

"Shall we?" he asked, holding out one

arm.

"We shall," Addie replied as she tucked her free arm in his.

The two chatted on the brief ride home, coming up with increasingly ridiculous possibilities for the pot-luck. By the time Robert pulled into her driveway, Addie couldn't stop laughing.

"Can you imagine the look on either of my aunt's faces if I showed up with the makings for s'mores?"

The image brought on a fresh wave of laughter. And that's how Jonah found them as he approached the car. He opened the back door, reaching for the girls' leashes.

"What did I miss?" he asked.

Addie just shook her head, unable to form words. Robert didn't do much better.

"S'mores," he blurted out before collapsing over the steering wheel in a renewed fit of laughter.

The look on Jonah's face only made her laugh harder.

"S'mores f-f-for the p-p-pot-luck!" she eked out before doubling over.

"Not sure they've gotten over the great nacho disaster of 2019. We might be pushing our luck," Jonah suggested, with a grin.

"No more. I can't breathe," she protested. She stumbled from the car before turning back to Robert. "Thank you so much for the ride home. I'll see you in the morning."

"Of course, my dear." Robert waved to Jonah. "Always a pleasure. I'll see you soon."

Jonah waved back, and they walked to the house after letting the girls stop to relieve themselves.

"It's hard to remember when he wasn't here," Jonah remarked as he held the door for her.

"Right? I know that's odd since I spent the first thirty-five years of my life not having a father, but it feels good having him here. He fits." She smiled at Jonah. "I'm so happy to have him here, especially at Christmas. It's our first Christmas," she said in a voice that cracked a bit at the end.

"First of many, Addy, first of many. Why don't you wash up? I brought dinner home with me. We can eat in front of the fire."

She leaned up on her tip-toes and kissed him.

"Sounds like a plan."

"And you'll have to tell me how s'mores seemed like a good idea," he joked.

"Give me five minutes."

Addie dashed into their bedroom and changed. She washed up and headed back out, her nose following the delicious smells of spicy food. She paused at the entrance to the living room, smiling at the sight of her two dogs prancing around the coffee table, noses in the air. Jonah sat on the couch and leaned forward, dishing food onto both of their plates.

"Don't start without me," Addie joked as she joined him.

"Never. The girls and I just had a chat about what Santa Paws might be bringing them for Christmas."

"Hmmm, let me guess. Maybe some treats? And some toys?"

They both laughed as the words sent both dogs into a twirling frenzy at their feet.

Lily sidled up to Addie nudging her hand with a cool nose. Addie ruffled her silky fur.

"Yes, my darling girl, Santa Paws will not forget you this year."

Gracey barked, making both humans laugh.

"Santa won't forget you either, silly goose," Jonah told her.

"If nothing else, Gertie will have t-r-e-a-t-s for them. She came by today to have the girls 'taste-test' a last minute new recipe. Needless to say, they both loved it."

"At least the girls are easy to please. I can't imagine what we're going to think up to bring on Christmas Eve," Jonah complained. "I guess s'mores aren't really an option."

Addie laughed at the little boy look on his face. Neither of them had any culinary skills.

"Come one, Jonah. How hard could this be? We are two intelligent, educated adults. Figuring out one pot-luck dinner contribution shouldn't be so hard."

"And yet it is," he mumbled around a

mouthful of moo shu pork.

She leaned back into the couch cushions with a sigh.

"I know. If only that was the toughest thing I had to worry about this Christmas."

"Hey! We got this, Addie. We'll figure out who this guy is and what he wants in plenty of time for Christmas," Jonah tried to assure her.

"Will we? I just want this Christmas to be like last year, when we didn't have some stupid mystery hanging over our heads." She leaned into him, wrapping her arms around his waist. "Remember how wonderful last year was? Our first Christmas together."

Jonah turned in her embrace and pressed a kiss into her hair.

"I do, honey. Of course I do. But I have it on good authority that this year will be even better. Just wait."

"Oh, you do, huh? And who told you this? Did a little bird whisper it to you?"

"No, but a certain pair of Shelties may have," he joked.

Addie watched Jonah love on the girls, stroking their silky heads. There was something about him tonight, something different. His eyes shone with excitement. And he almost seemed, well, nervous. The past few days, he seemed constantly in motion, edgy, not like himself at all.

Jonah flicked on the television and shocked her by switching to the Hallmark movie channel.

"This is how much I love you, Addie Foster. Grey texted me to make sure we watched nothing but 'sappy Christmas romance movies' tonight. His words, not mine."

Addie laughed, then clapped her hands when she looked at the television.

"Oh, I love this one. She sends a card and care package to this guy in the military overseas. And he reads it over and over again, and her words and kindness get him through the whole year. So when he gets out and ships back to America the next December, he decides to track her down." Addie sighed and hugged a Christmas throw pillow to her chest. "But soon after arriving in her small town, they meet accidentally. Their cute meet is adorable."

"Their cute what?" he asked.

"A 'cute meet' is a movie term where the hero and heroine meet in a cute manner, like bumping into each other or some sort of mistaken identity. It sets the tone for the rest of the movie. For these two, it's over an order of French fries each thinks belongs to them." Addie sighed. "If only real life were so easy."

"Meeting at a crime scene with you covered in someone's blood doesn't count, huh?"

"Not even a little," Addie joked. She hugged him a little harder. "But I wouldn't trade us for the world, terrible beginning or not."

"Right back at you!" He gave her a

smacking kiss before letting go of her. "So let's finish dinner and come up with our pot-luck contribution. Can't have that hanging over my head for the next two days."

"Agreed," Addie mumbled while digging into her dinner. Then something else occurred to her. "How's your Christmas shopping going? I'm pretty sure I know what you're getting for me."

Jonah fumbled his moo shu pork-laden fork halfway to his mouth. Food spilled everywhere. He grabbed for his napkin and almost upended his soda can.

Addie couldn't stop the laughter pouring out of her. Jonah was normally not the clumsy one of the two of them.

"What do you mean?" He finished cleaning up the mess and turned to her. "What I meant to say was, you couldn't possibly know what I've gotten for you."

Addie laughed again. She'd dropped only about a million hints. Starting last summer. If she couldn't wear flip flops, then snuggly winter boots were her next choice. She'd never had a pair of Uggs and wanted one. Badly! She'd even gone so far as to send him a screen shot of a pair she loved advertised on Black Friday. Surely, that was enough to make him understand how much she wanted them. And though he'd never acknowledged the text, she made sure Grey followed up with him on one of their infrequent "boys' nights out."

She smirked at Jonah. "Okay, then, I'm sure you're right."

She patted his hand for effect. Let him think she didn't know. She'd play along with his little charade, even so far as acting "surprised" on Christmas morning.

"If I were you, I'd be more concerned with your DIY gift for the exchange. Have you even started?"

"Ha! I'll have you know I'm done with mine. And whoever gets it will be pleased."

In truth, Addie had sweated bullets when DIY had been chosen as this year's theme. What did she know about how to DIY? Nothing! But Google and *Good Housekeeping* magazine had solved that dilemma. Addie had made half a dozen homemade glass ornaments. She filled each one with something different in all the lovely colors of Christmas. And best of all, they didn't look as though a toddler made them. So, yes, someone would be lucky to have her first ever (and possibly only) DIY Christmas gift.

Jonah cocked his head and studied her. Maybe he thought she was kidding?

"You made your gift? Really?"

"Yes, really. Those were the rules."

"Following the rules has never exactly been your strong suit, Addie," Jonah scoffed.

"What? I always follow the rules."

Even to her own ears it hadn't sounded convincing.

"You *always* follow the rules? As in, don't

interfere with an active police investigation. Maybe like the one involving your hairdresser. And that's just one example. I have plenty."

"Well, that's hardly fair bringing up Gwen's death. I thought you meant smaller, everyday rules, like no jaywalking. I'm good at those rules."

"Oh, so you're good at the everyday ones, just not so much the bigger, life-threatening ones. Is that your argument?" He softened his words with a grin.

"Exactly!" She grinned, knowing she'd won the argument. "And besides all that, no one messes with the Aunties. They said DIY, so DIY it is." She gave him a saucy grin. "I'd love to know what you came up with."

"That's for me to know and you to find out," Jonah teased.

"As it's only less than two days away, I think I can wait. Besides, first I have to figure out who the man is, what he wants, and how to stop him. Piece of cake!"

"And by *you,* you really mean *me*, right?"

She patted his hand. "Of course, Jonah."

Chapter Twelve

The sirens grew closer, but the maniacal gleam in the man's eyes dashed her hopes. As if he could read her thoughts, the man rapped his walking stick on the ground.

"Don't even think about it, young lady. He'll never get to you on time."

Before Addie could respond, the man lunged at her, pulling at her fleece gloves. For as old and frail as he appeared, he had a lot of strength. He grasped both of her hands in one of his while the other held the gun trained on her. His walking stick clattered to the floor.

"Take off your gloves," the man ordered.

"Wh-wh-what?"

His grip on her hands tightened in punishment.

"I ask the questions, not you. Now take off your gloves." He released her hands and pointed the *muzzle of the gun at her heart. "I won't ask again."*

Addie drew her fleece gloves off her shaking hands. She didn't understand what was happening but hoped doing as he asked would buy her some precious time; maybe enough for help to arrive.

"No!" the man screamed as he glanced at her hands. "Where is it?"

Unsure what he was talking about, but knowing she was out of time, Addie ducked to the floor. She felt the walking stick he'd dropped and grabbed it in her hands. He might shoot her, but she wasn't going out without a fight.

As she sprang up, wielding the heavy stick, a single gunshot shattered the quiet of the room. She waited for the pain.

"Ahhhhh," Adie cried as she tried to get away from the man. But she couldn't move. Something had her bound in place.

"Addie, you're okay," Jonah soothed from right next to her.

She opened her eyes and glanced around the room, happy to find her bedroom walls and not wherever she'd been in her nightmare. She looked at her hands and let out a half-laugh, half-sob when she realized the comforter "bound" her in place. She sat up and ran a shaky hand through her hair.

"Do you need water?" Jonah asked.

"Yes, please," she answered through very dry lips.

When Jonah left the room, Addie sighed and thought about the dream. Although it had frightened her, it also brought a sense of relief. She'd been through this enough to know the end was near, most likely today. Whatever needed to happen would happen today, and then she could get on with Christmas. That thought curled her lips.

"I didn't expect to find you smiling after the nightmare," Jonah commented and handed her a glass of ice water.

She gulped down half the glass before turning to him.

"The nightmare itself, and that creepy man, scared me. But tomorrow is Christmas Eve, and I happen to believe in the magic of Christmas." She raised a hand to rub the scruff on his jaw. "Everything will work out, Jonah. I have to believe that."

"Good! Glad to hear that. Natalie and I have been running down other patrons at the estate sales. Nothing's popped so far, but we still have some ground to cover. Speaking of which, I need to be out of the shower already."

He kissed her before heading into the bathroom.

The partially closed bedroom door swung open, admitting two smiling Shelties.

"Good morning, girls. Has Jonah fed you already?"

Both dogs whined and twirled in circles. Addie laughed at their antics.

"I'm sure he has, but you can keep me company while I make some coffee."

Addie got out of bed and stretched before heading down the hall. The girls danced at her feet, yipping at each other.

While her cup of coffee brewed, Addie grabbed a yogurt and some blueberries from the fridge. Some mornings, she remembered to be healthy. And considering how many calories she'd consume at the Aunties' over Christmas, yogurt became her best option. She sat at the table, eating her breakfast, and mulling over her day.

With kids out of school for the holiday, today was Christmas Craft Day at Smiling Dog Books. She had several different craft times, each for different age groups, planned throughout the day. Both Erin and Grey would be there to cover, while she worked with the kids. Or "rug rats," as Grey referred to them. Grey never hid his distaste of small children, at least not from Addie. Thankfully, he managed to appear civil to their parents.

Having things to do today, not to mention the crowds of last-minute shoppers she anticipated, helped Addie focus. One way or the other, this ended today.

Hopefully, not with her getting shot...

*****

Late that afternoon, Addie slipped into her office, shutting the door behind her. She collapsed into her desk chair to take a well-earned five-minute break. Digging through her desk, she found her bottle of ibuprofen and popped two with her Diet Mt. Dew. She loved crafts with the kids, and Christmas crafts were her favorite. Seeing their little faces light up as she read them a book while making paper ornaments to hang on their own trees made her day. But too many nights of disturbed sleep took its toll.

All day, even when busy with the kids, tension knotted the muscles of her neck. She kept waiting for the other shoe to drop, so to speak. She was sure today the man would show himself. And yet he hadn't. At least not yet. Reminding herself the nightmares had occurred in darkness brought relief. Dusk quickly approached this time of the year. She still had time to end this.

A quick, sharp knock on the door preceded Grey as he entered.

"Hiding from those beastly small children, are we?" He plopped down in one of her visitor chairs. "Can't blame you."

"Ha ha, very funny. The kids' craft hours are done for the day, as you well know. I just came back to rest for a moment." She shook the medication bottle. "And take some of these."

The smile slid from Grey's handsome face.

"Are you okay? Headache?"

"Yes, and yes. My broken sleep is catching up with me. You know how it is. Every time one of these things happens, I'm exhausted by the time it's over."

"I do. Have you eaten anything since breakfast?"

She shook her head.

"And since Christmas is in just a few days, I imagine you ate a healthy breakfast today. Right?"

"You know me too well," she sighed.

"Well, duh! We have been friends since single digits. Why don't I pop out and get you something?"

"That would be great, thanks. I don't even care what it is. Surprise me," she added.

Grey's mouth hung open.

"What? You never let me choose." He rushed closer to hold his hand to her forehead. "Are you feverish?" he joked.

"No," she responded with a laugh. "What I am, is hungry. I could eat my shoes about now. I already told Jonah I wouldn't be home for dinner, as it's the last full day before Christmas, so make this dinner. And since there are still a lot of children out there, I figured you'd rather go than stay."

"And you would be right. I'll be back before you can even miss me."

"But I miss you already."

"Right back at you," he replied before leaving.

Knowing she couldn't hide here any longer, especially with only Erin manning the store, Addie grabbed her soda bottle and left her office. She smiled at customers as she made her rounds. Although the crowd had thinned, the remaining number pleased her. Without even checking, Addie knew this had been her best holiday season to date. The knowledge that she was actually living her dream made her smile.

How many people could say that?

Icy tendrils down her spine replaced the warm glow of that knowledge. She heard the bells over the door at the same moment she caught sight of *him*. People between her and the door blocked most of her vision, but Addie caught sight of the overcoat and a hand on top of a walking stick. It had to be him. The hairs standing up on the back of her neck didn't lie.

Without another thought, Addie raced for the door. He wasn't getting away again. Not this time! She ignored a cry from a startled Erin at the counter and sprinted through the door. The last dying rays of the sun were almost history, and the chill bit through Addie's thin sweater vest. She pulled on the fleece gloves she had in her pocket as she walked to the corner. Looking up and down the street, Addie couldn't find the man. She clenched her hands into fists at her side and stepped to the corner.

Faint movement to her right caught her attention. *Was that the hem of an overcoat flapping in the wind?* She started down the side street to check. As she walked, Addie pulled out her phone and called Jonah. It went right to voicemail. She groaned at her luck as she waited through the message. At the beep, Addie whispered into her phone what was happening and where she was. She knew Jonah would not be pleased about this. Nothing she could do about that now.

The click of a door shutting dragged her from her musing. Addie looked up, realizing she stood in front of an empty storefront. What once had held Gallagher Family Jewelers now stood empty. She'd hadn't been in the business since she was a little girl. Aunt Beatrice had taken her a few times. She remembered staring into the glass display cases in wonder at the beautiful items within. Her favorites had always been the older, vintage pieces.

Glass display cases! That's what reflected in her nightmare. A chill that had nothing to do with the temperature swept through her body. Knowing what she had to do, Addie approached the door. She placed her hand on the ornate golden door handle. As she knew it would, the door opened easily toward her. She slid through, gently closing the door behind her. No use alerting him to her presence just yet. She crept along the wall, willing her eyes to adjust to the lack of light inside the old store. Addie held her breath when a floorboard creaked under her foot. But it was too late.

"How nice of you to join me, Miss Foster," came a voice from the shadows. A hideous laugh followed, its hollow ring sending a torrent of fresh chills down her spine. "Not that you had much of a choice."

Addie pressed herself against the wall. Maybe if she bought a little time for Jonah, or any of the Ocean Grove PD to arrive, she'd be all right.

Before she could shrink far enough into the shadows, a hand snaked out, wrapping itself around her wrist like a manacle. "Where do you think you're going?" Venom dripped from the disembodied voice, with all traces of humor gone.

Chapter Thirteen

Addie breathed in slowly and deeply. *Stay focused!*

"Who are you, and what do you want?" she asked the man still hiding in the shadows.

He stepped forward, coming into the dim light filtering in from outside. The dirty windows spoke of neglect of what had once been a thriving business.

"It seems only fair, Addie Foster, since I know who you are."

The sound of her name coming from his lips with such venom intensified the chills racing down her spine. She said nothing, hoping he would continue.

"My name is Julian Gallagher, and this is or was my family's business."

He spread his arm wide to emphasize his point. But the green eyes of the dragon on his walking stick stole her attention. They seemed to glow in the murky light. Addie closed her eyes for a second to clear that image.

Get ahold of yourself!

"That tells me who you are, Mr. Gallagher, but it does not tell me anything else. What do you want from me?"

"Do you know how long I've searched for this? Do you?" The man's voice reached an almost ear-splitting decibel. "Only to find out someone beat me to it! Well, I won't stand for it." He shoved a long, bony hand into Addie's face. "Give it to me now."

She jumped back from the gnarled hand, with its twisted and deformed knuckles.

"If I had any idea what you were talking about, I'd be happy to return it."

"Well, if you don't have it, then one of those men must. I don't have all day, young lady. And I am losing my patience. I need it now."

He banged the floor beneath their feet with his cane. Although he appeared and sounded elderly, the force of the cane banging belied a much younger man. Addie did her best to shrink back away from him before he decided to use the cane on her.

Almost as though he'd read her mind, the man raised it again. This time, the handle appeared in the single source of weak light. The head of a dragon with glowing green eyes stopped in front of Addie's face. For a moment, she couldn't draw her eyes from it.

"No matter to me which of them has it. What's mine is mine, and you'll take me to him," he growled at her.

The dim light shone on the metal of a small gun in his hand. Although the dream had warned her of this, Addie gasped. If only she knew what he was talking about, then maybe she could figure a way out of this mess. Knowing she was on her own at the moment, Addie slowed her breathing. She focused only on the man and small but lethal looking gun in his hand.

"Maybe we could turn on a light, pull up a chair, and then you could explain to me what it is you're talking about. You keep saying 'it,' but I have no idea what it might be."

But if the hardening of his features meant anything, her attempt had failed.

"Do you think I'm stupid, young lady?" he growled at Addie.

"O-o-of c-c-course n-n-not," she replied, clenching both hands together. She didn't want to show any fear. Or at least any more fear.

"One of them bought it at an estate sale in South Carolina last weekend." The man stopped, cocked his head, and stared at Addie, as though trying to figure out a riddle. "Humph, maybe you don't know. Neither here nor there. He has what's mine. And I will get it back."

Before Addie could reply, the man closed the space between them until the barrel of his gun stabbed into her ribs. Time was running out.

"Enough!" the man cried as he whipped the cane through the air next to her, smashing the glass display case into smithereens.

Addie cried out as a shard of glass nicked her face.

"That's the least of your worries. I'll ask you one more time, young lady. Where is it?"

"Don't you think I'd tell you if I knew?" she cried out in the murky darkness.

"I don't know why you're lying to me," he bellowed. "It won't save you."

The pressure of the gun in her ribs increased, driving home his point. Addie bit back a sob. Tomorrow was Christmas Eve. She wanted to be with Jonah and Grey and her family, celebrating. Hot tears burned her eyes, but she refused to let them fall. She wouldn't give him the satisfaction. Her mind whirled, seeking an escape from this situation.

Just then a siren pierced the quiet of the room. Hope stirred within her as the sound grew closer. Someone was coming. Jonah was coming. He would save her from this man.

But icy tendrils of fear gripped her at the sound of the man's maniacal laughter.

"You really think he's going to save you? Your detective friend? Not without getting what I want. What I need! Maybe he'll get here in time to watch the life bleed out of you instead."

As the man's laughter filled the room, Addie knew he was losing his grip on reality.

She might not have until Jonah got here. *Think! Keep him talking!*

"Why is this item so important to you? You never said."

"It's been passed down in my family for generations. Over one hundred and fifty years ago, my who knows how many great grandfathers gave it to woman he loved. Since that time, it was passed along with each generation, bringing with it continued luck and prosperity for the whole family."

Addie watched him stare into middle space with his lips still moving but no sound coming out. He looked as though he was deep in conversation. With whom was anyone's guess.

"If it brings wealth and good luck, what happened to this store?"

The words left her mouth before Addie could stop them. Mr. Gallagher whirled on her.

"Exactly! What a great question. Maybe we should ask my brother, Grant." Spittle flew from his mouth, and his eyes grew scarier. "Oh, that's right, we can't! Because he killed himself."

Addie gasped, her hand flying to cover her mouth. Maybe the loss of his brother had been too big a one. Maybe it was been the proverbial last straw.

"I'm so sorry for your loss, Mr. Gallagher."

"Don't waste your breath. Grant was a coward who took the easy way out," he seethed.

"Oh, I don't know about that. Suicide is

132

never the easy choice," Addie responded.

A harsh laugh holding no humor ripped from the deepest part of him.

"It was for him. You see, Grant liked the ponies a bit too much. In fact, that man would bet on our own mother's death if he thought he could turn a profit. And he did well for a long time. Until he didn't. And then a certain type of person came after him to collect his debts. And since my brother values his kneecaps, he sold a bunch of family things. Including the ring."

"So the thing you seek is a ring?"

"Not just any ring, young lady. It's a Claddagh ring from the nineteenth century."

"And you believe someone I know bought it?"

The sirens had stopped. Help must be nearby. She hadn't given an exact location, but they would find her. Hopefully, sooner rather than later.

"Let's not be coy, Miss Foster. Either Detective Jonah Wolfe or Greyson Waverly has what is rightfully mine. And I mean to have it back."

Before Addie could respond, the man lunged at her, pulling at her fleece gloves. For as old and frail as he appeared, he had a lot of strength. He grasped both of her hands in one of his while the other held the gun trained on her. His walking stick clattered to the floor.

"Take off your gloves," the man ordered.

"Wh-wh-what?"

His grip on her hands tightened in punishment.

"I ask the questions, not you. Now take off your gloves." He released her hands and pointed the muzzle of the gun at her heart. "I won't ask again."

Addie drew her fleece gloves off her shaking hands. She hoped doing as he asked would buy her some precious time; maybe enough for help to arrive.

"No! You really don't have it," the man screamed as he glanced at her hands. "Where is it?"

Knowing she was out of time, Addie dropped to the floor. She felt the walking stick he'd discarded and grabbed it in her hands. He might shoot her, but she wasn't going out without a fight.

As she sprang up, wielding the heavy stick, a single gunshot shattered the quiet of the room. She waited for the pain.

Chapter Fourteen

"Addie?" Jonah's voice rang out in the eerie silence after the deafening racket of the gunshot.

"I'm okay, Jonah," she cried before falling into his arms, oblivious to the crush of bodies entering the space.

"You have to stop scaring me like this," he gently admonished her.

Addie nodded her head against his chest. After taking a few breaths, she glanced down at the floor behind her. Mr. Gallagher lay oh so still on the floor. A puddle of his blood surrounded him.

"Is h-h-he d-d-dead?" she asked before burying her face again.

Jonah pulled her into his arms and walked her away from the body. She felt him nod to someone but couldn't care less about what happened around her. She wanted this whole nightmare to end.

"Baby, let me take you outside," he whispered.

She didn't flinch when he picked her up in his arms and walked out of the building. The chattering of her teeth had nothing to do with the chilly air.

"Addie! Where are you?"

The frantic call sounded from two different directions. She bowed her head, knowing both Grey and Robert had been frantic. She felt a hand touch her shoulder from behind.

"I only left for a few minutes to get something for dinner," Grey scolded.

"I'm not sure how much my heart can take," Robert added.

That made her laugh; great, big cackles more sob than laughter wracked her body. The former spy or whatever he'd been was shaken by her brush with death?

"I'm so sorry," she whispered to Jonah, but also to the other men in her life.

"I know," he responded with a kiss to her forehead before gently sliding her down to her own feet. "Do you feel up to answering a few questions?"

"Yes, of course," she answered through chattering teeth.

"Here you go, my dear," Robert said as he wrapped her in his overcoat.

Knowing they all had questions, Addie told them everything Mr. Gallagher had said in the abandoned shop. Even the short speech seemed more than she could handle. She swayed on her feet as she finished telling them.

"Grey or Robert, please go get your car and take Addie to the station. She'll need to give an official statement. I'll be along behind you after I finish up here."

Addie stared at him.

"Don't you have to give the chief your weapon? Because you, you know, shot him."

"I never drew my weapon, Addie. One of our officers arrived about thirty seconds before I did. He took the shot," Jonah explained.

"I th-th-thought Mr. Gallagher shot me. I waited for the pain. Your officer saved my life." A silly grin that spoke more of adrenalin than humor stole across her face. "Although, I was prepared to bash in his head with his own walking stick."

"Good to know," Jonah said in a deeper, rougher voice. "And let's not even put the idea of you getting shot into the universe, shall we?"

The sound of tires squealing on the pavement drew their attention. Grey slid to a stop at the curb. He jumped out and took Addie by the hand.

"I'm ready when you are."

Addie nodded.

"Oh, what about the girls? And the shop? I have to get back there."

Robert stepped up placing a hand on her shoulder.

"I'll see to it, my dear. You take care of things at the station. I'll close up the shop and take the girls to your house."

Relief flooded through her, followed quickly by gratitude. She was so lucky to have these people in her life.

"Thank you, uh, Dad."

The smile on his face told Addie how he felt about that. She'd struggled with calling him by anything but his first name. But he was taking care of her, worrying about her, like a father did.

Then a terrible thought crossed her mind. She turned to Jonah.

"I don't want the ring. I'm sorry, but after what just happened, I'd feel terrible wearing it."

The color drained form Jonah's face in front of her eyes.

"It's a shame he had to ruin it for us. I've always loved Claddagh rings." She sighed.

A small smile appeared on his handsome face.

"I didn't buy you a Claddagh ring, Addie. He must have gotten confused."

"Oh, thank goodness," she cried. The stress of the day had caught up with her as sobs wracked her frame.

Grey took her icy cold hands in his and rubbed them.

"Come along, Addie. Let's get this over

with."

She nodded and let him lead her to his car.

*****

Many hours later, Jonah opened the front door and ushered her inside. She still wore Robert's, her father's, overcoat. Despite the heat in the police station, Addie felt a chill down to her marrow.

"What can I make you for dinner, Addie?" Jonah asked.

She shook her head. Natalie had brought her hot chocolate and some peanut butter crackers at the station. And though that was all she'd eaten since breakfast, the thought of food turned her stomach.

"No, thank you, Jonah. Would it be the worst thing if I just wanted a hot shower and sleep?"

Her dogs crowded her feet, each yipping for attention.

"Make that a hot shower, my bed, and some quality time with the family."

"Not even close to the worst thing. Sounds like a plan. Why don't you go take that shower, and I'll let the girls out and lock up?"

Tears flooded her eyes at his sweetness. She threw her arms around him.

"I don't know what I ever did to deserve you, Jonah, but I thank the universe every day."

She felt the tears flow down her cheeks and did nothing to stop them. It had been a crazy couple of days.

Jonah gathered her closer. "Are you kidding me? I'm the lucky one." He placed a kiss on her head before releasing her. "Go get ready for bed. I won't be long."

"Thank you," she whispered. "For everything."

Addie walked straight into their bathroom, stripping clothes as she went. She would never be warm again after tonight. Turning on the shower as hot as she could stand, she washed her face and brushed her teeth before jumping in. And then she stood there, allowing the steaming water to wash away the events of the day.

And that's when a smile started to form. They'd done it! The bad man, Julian Gallagher, had been stopped. There wouldn't be another nightmare tonight. She could get a nice long winter's nap, as the book goes, before returning to her bookstore tomorrow for the very last shopping day before Christmas.

And then her smile grew even bigger because once she closed Smiling Dog Books at four in the afternoon, as she always did on Christmas Eve, the fun would really begin. There would be more food than any of them could finish, a gift exchange game to survive, Christmas carols to be sung. The thought of all those things made her heart lighter than it had been for days. But best of all, there would be another Christmas Eve spent with family and friends.

Chapter Fifteen

"Are we ready for this?" Jonah joked as he pulled into the Aunties' driveway.

"I'm not sure we can ever be 'ready,' but I am excited."

Addie turned to look at the girls in the back seat of her car. In that canine way, the girls started yipping and getting restless the moment Jonah made the turn onto Sea Grass Way. Now that Jonah had turned off the car, the girls could barely contain themselves.

"Someone's happy," Jonah murmured. His words were mostly drowned out by the cacophony of barking.

"Well, at least they're ready." She grinned at Jonah. "Let's do this!"

He caught her gaze and squeezed Addie's gloved hand. "I'm more ready than I've ever been."

With that mysterious statement, Jonah got out and opened the back seat. Addie remained where she was for a moment to watch him with the girls, and Jonah walked them into the grass to give them a chance for one last potty break before heading inside. Even now, he paced back and forth while the girls frolicked at the end of their flexible leads. A thin layer of snow had fallen overnight, very uncommon for their seaside town, and the girls rushed back and forth in it. Their pawprints obliterated the virgin canvas of the yard, and Jonah continued to pace. Odd, but she'd ask him about it later.

Addie finally got out and grabbed their stuff from the back of her car. Between the gifts and their contribution for the pot-luck, she could barely close the hatch.

"Here we go," she called over her shoulder as she made her way up the drive.

Addie didn't even make the porch when the front door flew open. Out came Robert, with Grey on his heels.

"You look lovely, my dear. Let me help you with those," Robert offered, taking two reusable grocery bags from her hands. "Do you have more in the car?"

The girls bounded up the stairs, bouncing around Grey. He reached down and unclipped their leashes. After getting a quick pat from him, Lily and Gracey raced inside.

"Wait until the girls get a sniff of all the food in there. They'll be in doggy heaven," Grey told them.

"Is everyone already here?" Jonah asked. "We needed to go home first after Addie closed the store.

"Yep, y'all are the last ones," Grey confirmed. "And since I was here first, I call dibs on Gertie's chocolate malted fudgy peppermint pie."

"You don't get the whole thing, Grey," scolded the baker herself. Gertie joined them closing the door behind them and taking their coats. "Yes, you were here first, so you get a *piece*."

"But, Gertie," Grey whined. "That one's my favorite of yours ever. I need more than a piece."

Addie burst out laughing at his antics. "You forgot to stomp your foot, Grey."

"Did you forget about my chocolate-bourbon pecan pie, Grey?" Gertie asked.

"And we can't forget your world-famous sweet potato pie with marshmallow meringue," Jonah added.

"I wouldn't go so far as to say 'world-famous,' Jonah, although I appreciate the compliment."

"I would," he replied, rubbing his stomach.

"Hey, partner, about time you got here. Miss Beatrice and Miss Clementine have already plied Sean and I with their 'special recipe' egg nog. We may need a ride home later," Natalie told them.

Addie laughed and shook her head.

"My bad, Natalie, I probably should have warned y'all. Their egg nog is to be sipped slowly. Very slowly. I hope you've eaten something."

"Is that my great niece I hear? Finally!" bellowed Aunt Clementine as she joined them all. "What took you so long? Did you stop to get nachos?"

Clementine cackled and slapped her knee at her own joke.

"Looks like someone else may have sampled the egg nog," Jonah joked.

"Well, maybe if you'd gotten here on time, we wouldn't have had to start without you, Jonah," Beatrice scolded.

"There's plenty to go around. No need to worry," Clementine announced, swaying ever so slightly. "Now that the gang's all here, let's get to dinner. Everything is set up as a buffet on the sideboard." She turned and stared at Addie over her glasses, which had slipped to the end of her nose. "Everything except what you and Jonah brought. I'm going to assume you didn't make it nachos two years in a row."

Addie felt her face heat. *Would she ever live that down?*

"You know what they say happens when you assume, Clementine," Grey snarked.

Addie held in a snicker as her elderly aunt fixed Grey with a stare. She almost couldn't hold it in as Grey paled before her eyes.

"And you're about to find out what happens to people who get a little big for their britches, young man. I'll give you a hint. You'll be going to bed hungry tonight." Clementine held his gaze for a beat longer. "And we wouldn't want that, would we, Grey?"

"No, ma'am, we would not," he replied in the smallest voice Addie had heard from him since the infamous day he lost control of his dirt bike in her prized rose garden.

Everyone else burst into laughter at his tone and the red seeping into his face. Addie couldn't find it in her heart to feel sorry for him. Everyone, Grey especially, knew better than to sass either of the Aunties.

"And now that that's settled, everyone wash up for dinner," Aunt Clementine commanded.

Addie and Jonah showed Natalie and her fiancé to the first-floor powder room before taking the stairs up to use a different bathroom.

"Did you see the look on Grey's face? You could tell the exact moment he figured out he'd crossed the line," Jonah snickered. "Remind me never to get anywhere near it."

After washing her hands, Addie pulled a ribbon from her pocket, pulling her wild curls off her face. Jonah smiled from behind her in the mirror.

"Your mom's earrings look great with that sweater."

"Thank you! I really should wear them more often." She reached up and touched one of the ruby stones. "I feel closer to her when I wear them." She sighed. "I miss her every day, but I miss her more at Christmas."

"I know you do, honey. I wish I could have met her." He kissed her temple.

"She would have loved you. Just like I do."

"That's all I need for Christmas," he whispered.

"We'd better go before they eat all the food."

Jonah took her hand and held it all the way downstairs. Addie dashed to the front door, where they'd left their bags. She pulled a covered dish from one and handed it to Jonah. From the second bag, she pulled the rest of their contribution arranged on a platter decorated with holly.

In the dining room, they found everyone milling about and filling their plates with various choices. Addie found a space and placed her things down.

"This is why we were late, everyone. For the first time ever, I made something instead of buying it. Ta da!"

She stepped back to show off her spinach dip and crudites.

"Looks great, but will it kill us?" asked Grey.

"I would think you'd learned your lesson

earlier, young man," Clementine scolded. She stepped forward, grabbed a strip of red bell pepper, and scooped a healthy amount of the dip before popping it in her mouth.

Addie's heart pounded as she, and everyone else, waited for the final verdict.

Clementine smiled from ear to ear. "There's hope for you yet, dear. Now, everyone, dig in."

Laughter, conversation, and the sounds of eating filled the air for the next hour. Addie's heart swelled as she looked around the table at family, friends both old and new, and of course Jonah, her one true love. Life might get crazy at times (some times more than others), but she wouldn't change hers for anything. Everything she needed was right here.

She felt a hand on her shoulder, and Addie turned toward her father. He raised his hand to her ear, touching the ruby earring she wore. She smiled.

"Do you like these? They belonged to my mother. Clementine and Beatrice gave them to me when I graduated from college. They had given them to my mother when she graduated from college. My mother loved rubies."

"I remember," her father said. He cleared his throat. "One rainy afternoon, long ago, your mother and I whiled away half a day at The National Gallery of Art. We drifted through the exhibits, one more lovely than the previous. Your mother became enthralled with a watercolor by Robert Stewart of a ruby vase. As we were about to leave, she dragged me back to it in order to 'commit to memory,' as she said." He shook his head. His eyes held a far-off look. "On our last day together before the semester ended and she had to return home, I gave her a scarf…"

Addie gasped.

"You gave her a ruby-colored silk scarf. It was her favorite. She wore it on special occasions, much as I do these earrings." Addie swallowed a lump growing in her throat. "I was just telling Jonah that wearing these always makes me feel closer to her."

"You wear them well, my dear. It's nice to know you have a piece of Julia to remind you." Robert wiped a hand over his eyes. "Her death at such a young age was a tragedy. I'd always hoped," he stopped and cleared his throat. "Never mind the ramblings of a foolish old man."

"You're neither old nor foolish, Dad. Please go on," Addie encouraged.

"You favor her, you know." He ran a hand over her ebony curls. "What I tried to say was that I had always hoped, against all odds, that Julia and I would find our way back to each other. Someday. Somehow." He swallowed hard. "Don't let time slip away from you, my dear. Don't have regrets."

Addie brushed a tear away from her cheek.

"I try not to."

"And now the moment everyone has been anticipating! Gift exchange time!" Grey yelled.

His loud voice and childlike enthusiasm broke the spell wrapped around Addie and her father. She squeezed his hand before turning away.

"I thought the moment everyone waited for was dessert, including my pies," Gertie cried.

"That's *my* favorite moment," Jonah exclaimed.

"Suck up!" Grey called with laughter in his voice.

"Boys! Pipe down, please," Beatrice requested. When she had everyone's attention, she spoke again. "Before dessert, to give us a chance to digest a bit, we're going to play our gift exchange game. Everyone, bring your chair into the living room, please. And before we get started, maybe a fire in the fireplace."

Everyone did as instructed, Addie noticed. Even Sean and Natalie, the first-timers, didn't dare disobey one of the Aunties. They made a large circle of the chairs, all facing inward. Robert knelt by the fire, coaxing it to life. She smiled at the pile of presents, all homemade per the rules, under the soaring Christmas tree. Life didn't get any better than this.

After a few minutes of chaos, people took their seats. Grey stood with a flourish to announce the rules.

"For anyone who hasn't played this one before, this is how it works. Everyone sits in the circle of chairs, facing each other. We start by choosing two gifts from the pile, and they get passed to your right." Grey held up his right hand. "That's this one, for anyone who might be confused."

"Very funny, Grey, now get on with it," Jonah called, tongue firmly in cheek.

"As I was saying, the gifts are passed to your right. Sean has valiantly agreed to be our official timer. He will play a Christmas song on his phone. When the music stops, whoever still has a gift in their hands wins it. Got it?"

"Poor Sean doesn't get a gift," Natalie complained good-naturedly.

"I already have you. What else could I possibly want?" her fiancé commented.

A chorus of "Oohs" and "Aahs" rose in the crowd with the exception of one person making a sound very similar to that of a cat coughing up a hairball.

"Really, Grey?" Addie admonished.

"Yes, really, from the cynical corner. But don't fret over Sean. As timer, he gets to choose any gift he wants from the pile before we start. Then with each round, the winners will reveal the gifts they received and leave the circle before the next round begins. Now, are there any questions?" Grey looked around. When no one else spoke up, he nodded. "Okay then, Sean, pick your gift."

The firefighter, who also had a healthy sense of humor, pawed through all the gifts, even picking up one or two to shake, before finally choosing a brightly-colored gift bag. He pulled out tissue paper and held aloft a pair of salt and pepper shakers with Rudolph and Santa painted on them.

"Nicely done, whoever painted these," Sean said. "They'll look great in our new home."

Natalie clapped her hands. "Ooh, I get two gifts, then!"

Everyone laughed. Sean held aloft his phone. He chose two gifts from the pile, handing one to Grey and the other to Clementine.

"Here we go!"

The opening strains of Perry Faith's "We Need a Little Christmas" filled the air. The two gifts were passed around. After thirty seconds or so, Sean stopped the music. The gifts were won by Gertie and Erin. Both women jumped up and down, squealing.

"You don't even know what you won," remarked Grey. "It could be something Addie made. Or worse yet, Jonah."

"Ha ha, very funny," Addie answered. "Whoever gets mine will be pleasantly surprised." She pointed a thumb at Jonah. "Not sure I can say the same for him," she joked. "Hopefully, he did better than he wraps."

Jonah chuckled. "She's got me there. I do use a lot of tape."

Gertie held her gift aloft. "Well, let's see

what I won. Not a lot of tape, so probably not from Jonah," she joked. She unwrapped the box and opened it to reveal a small wreath decorated with holly and seashells. "I love this!" she cried.

Erin clapped. "I'm so glad! I made that."

"Thank you, Erin. Now open yours."

Erin grinned and shook the gift bag.

"Hope it's not fragile," Grey joked.

She stuck her tongue out at him before pulling out festive-colored tissue paper. She held aloft a trio of small sachets. Each was made of a material depicting different scenes from Christmas.

"I filled them with different scents, dear. There's lavender, cedar, and cinnamon. I hope you like them, Erin," Aunt Beatrice advised.

Erin crossed the room and hugged Beatrice, bringing a huge smile to the older woman's face.

"I love them, Aunt Beatrice! Maybe you could show me how to make them sometime. I know my mom would love them, too. Her birthday's in March."

"I'd be happy to, my dear."

Addie smiled at the blush of pleasure on her Auntie's cheeks.

"Okay, you two, out of the circle," Grey ordered.

The two women laughed as they removed their gifts and chairs from the circle.

Several more rounds followed, with each person loving their home made gift until all that remained were Jonah and Addie. They grabbed the last two gifts, and Sean played Mariah Carey's "All I Want for Christmas is You." Addie laughed as she and Jonah faced each other and passed the last two gifts back and forth to each other. This went on until she saw Jonah nod to Sean, and the music stopped.

"Hey!" Addie laughed. "That's hardly fair. This game is rigged."

The others joined in laughing.

"Normally, I'd say the woman should go first, but Jonah was lucky enough to get my gift. Jonah, tear that bad boy open!" Grey commanded.

"I can hardly wait," Jonah replied in the driest tone possible.

Addie sat her gift bag on her lap and watched with everyone else as Jonah started to open his gift. Playing to his audience, he first shook it near his ear.

"With Grey, one can't be too careful." He lifted the bag again, grinning. "Feels heavy."

"For the love of all things Beyoncé, open it already," Grey whined.

"Keep your pants on, Grey!" Aunt Clementine yelled.

Jonah fished around and pulled out a mason jar decorated with a red and gold ribbon. He glanced at the tag and read aloud, "Citrus sugar scrub."

The entire room broke into laughter, Jonah and Grey included.

"Clearly, I expected a female to win this," Grey explained.

Addie held her bag aloft. "I'll trade you! I love anything citrusy. Besides, this feels pretty light."

"No trades!" Grey shouted. "I may not have mentioned it earlier, but it's in the rules."

"Spoil sport!" Addie cried.

She noticed Sean had started the song again but didn't mention it. "All I Want for Christmas is You" had always been a favorite of hers, especially since she now had Jonah.

"I can't wait to see what I got," she exclaimed, lifting up the bag. She then leaned forward and kissed Jonah. "But I already have everything I need."

The women in the crowd applauded while Jonah's cheeks pinked up.

"Good to know, since you're stuck with my DIY gift," he joked.

"Poor Addie," Grey sympathized.

"I'm not afraid," she said in a purposely shaky voice. "Okay, maybe a little."

Addie pulled out a handful of tissue paper. Her hand closed over what felt like a small box. She grasped it and lifted out a small, square velvet box. Her heart beat wildly, like that of a hummingbird. Her hands shook for real. She held the box in the palm of her hand and looked up to find Jonah on one knee in front of her.

"I have the feeling you broke the rules,

Jonah. This isn't DIY."

"You caught me, Addie. And now I have a question for you," he replied.

Chapter Sixteen

"Every time I asked Mom how she knew Dad was the one for her, she'd say the same thing. 'I just knew.' Same with my sisters and their husbands. I never believed them. I didn't understand their answer. And then one day I answered a frantic call about a woman in distress. The caller…"

"Ooh, that would be me," Grey interjected.

"Yes, Grey, that would be you," Jonah practically growled.

Everyone laughed, but Addie continued to stare into Jonah's dark chocolate eyes. She saw warmth and passion, fidelity, and the promise of a future.

"As I was saying, I arrived on scene to find a woman covered in blood and babbling."

"That would be me," Addie said in a

small, shaky voice.

"Yes, Addie, that would be you. And I knew she wasn't some crazy killer, despite all the blood. She was sweet and more than a little sassy."

"She gets that from me," Clementine exclaimed.

"And me," added Beatrice.

Jonah laughed.

"Can we focus, please?" He took both of Addie's hands in his own. "And soon, I knew a few more things about you. I knew you were smart and capable. I knew you gave everything you are to those you love. I knew you could make me laugh without even trying." He cleared his throat. "And above all else, I just knew. As my family had told me."

A shaky half-laugh, half-sob sounded from Addie. She pulled her hands from his and swiped at the tears coursing down her cheeks.

"So now there's only one more thing I need to know." He took her hands in his again. "Adelaide Foster, will you make me the happiest, luckiest man alive and agree to be my wife?"

Addie stared into his eyes again. Saw the one brow bisected with the decades-old scar lift. And her voice no longer shook when she answered.

"Of course I will, Jonah Wolfe. Nothing could make me happier!"

Jonah let out a huge breath and leaned in

to seal the deal with a kiss.

"Maybe you should look at the ring, Addie, before deciding," cackled Aunt Clementine.

"Oh, the ring. I forgot about the ring!" she cried.

Jonah chuckled. "Life with you will never be boring."

As she had before, Addie wondered what Jonah would choose for her. She opened the lid of the box and gasped. There, nestled in a bed of black velvet, sat the most beautiful ring she'd ever seen. A center round ruby sat enclosed by swirling delicate leaves in a platinum setting. The vintage look made her heart sing.

"Allow me," Jonah said. He pulled the ring from its box and slid it on her left hand. "I've spent over a year looking for this. Almost since our first official date. I had no idea other than a ruby but knew I'd know it when I saw it. Just as I knew about you. And last weekend, I found this."

"You went to an estate sale for me?" Addie cried.

"I'd go to the depths of Hell for you, Addie. All I ever wanted was to make you happy."

She smiled through her tears.

"You've done that and so much more." Addie glanced at the ruby ring now on her hand. "This matches my earrings. My mom's earrings. Oh, Jonah!" Her words broke off on a sob.

Jonah stood and pulled her up and into his arms. The rest of the party swirled around them.

"You've done well, lad," Robert said as he clapped Jonah on the back.

Jonah looked into Addie's eyes and wiped away the remaining tears.

"I certainly have," he murmured.

The End & Merry Christmas

ALSO BY KIMBERLEY O'MALLEY

COZY MYSTERIES
The Addie Foster Series
Book 1: Death Comes in Threes
http://bit.ly/KOMcozy1
Book 2: Dyeing for Change
http://bit.ly/Addie2KOM
Book 3: Murder by Numbers
http://bit.ly/AddieBook3
Book 4: Angel of Death http://bit.ly/Addie4
Book 5: Death by Chocolate
http://bit.ly/Addie5KOM

CONTEMPORARY ROMANCES
The Windsor Falls Series
Book 1: Coming Home
http://bit.ly/ComingHomeKOM
Book 2: Taking Chances
http://bit.ly/TakingCHancesKOM
Book 3: Second Chances
http://bit.ly/2ndChancesKOM
Book 4: Saving Quinn http://bit.ly/SavingQuinn
Book 5: Finding Kat http://bit.ly/FindingKat
Book 6: Coming Back
http://bit.ly/FInalWindsorFalls

The Palm Harbor Series
Book 1: The One that (Almost) Got Away
https://bit.ly/JamieKOM

ACKNOWLEDGMENTS

Writing has always been therapy for me. And this book isn't any different. After having total knee replacement (on my birthday no less), I needed something to keep me occupied and my mind off of the pain and difficulty. So, two days post op, this book was born. I wanted to write a Christmas book. I wanted to laugh while doing so. I accomplished both goals. I managed all thirty thousand plus words in less than a month. Of course, this begs the question why can't I always do this?

My readers and FB friends are simply the best!! They sent me cards and messages, checked in on me, made me laugh! I am so very grateful for each and every one of you. This book is my Christmas gift to you!!!

Margie Greenhow, PA extraordinaire, keeps me in line and on track. She nudges, cajoles, and sometimes shoves me into new adventures and undertakings. And I am a better person for it. Thank you!

Every author thinks they're brilliant. And then they think everything they write is pure...you get the idea. And that's why we have editors; people to keep us from slitting out wrists. And I'm lucky enough to have a few. Thank you to Karen Boston and Chelly Hoyle Peeler. You guys have a tough job.

Rebecca Pau of The Final Wrap is my brilliant cover designer, whom I love so very much. She always knows just what I want, and need, without my having to say it. Which is a good thing, as I'm terrible at putting my vision for my covers into words. You've never steered me wrong, and I cannot imagine anyone else creating my covers. Thank you for yet another gorgeous cover!

Molly & Callie, my Shetland Sheepdogs, are the inspiration for Gracey and Lily. They are truly my fur babies. Somedays I like them more than I do my human ones. They're always there at my side, with a lick or a woof to encourage me.

And, always, there's my family! They are at the center of everything I do.

HOW TO HELP AN
INDIE AUTHOR

Thank you for reading 'Twas the Mystery Before Christmas. I know you have millions of books to choose from, so thank for choosing mine.

So, here's one more favor...reviews, reviews, reviews! Even if you didn't fall in love with this book, please take the time to review it on Amazon, Goodreads and/or Book Bub. Reviews are so much more important than you could ever imagine.

ABOUT THE AUTHOR

Kimberley O'Malley is a transplant to Charlotte, North Carolina from the frozen North. She is learning to say y'all but draws the line at sweet tea. Sarcasm is an art form in her world. She writes small town Contemporary romances and hilarious Cozy Mysteries. When not writing, she is a full-time nurse and part-time soccer Mom, but not necessarily in that order. She shares her life with an amazing husband of more than 25 years, two teenagers, and two very sweet Shetland Sheepdogs, Molly & Callie.

To ensure you're up to date with all the shenanigans and news, visit the link to follow along with my monthly newsletter: http://eepurl.com/dgonEX

ARE YOU FOLLOWING THE AUTHOR?

Facebook - https://www.facebook.com/KOMalley67/

Instagram - https://www.instagram.com/kimberleyomalley67/

Twitter - https://twitter.com/K_OMalley67

Website - www.kimberleyomalley.com

Amazon Author Bio - www.amazon.com/author/kimberleyomalley

Good Reads Profile - http://bit.ly/grKOM

Book Bub Profile - http://bit.ly/bookbubKOM